# Golden BOY

## E. DAVIES

Publisher's Note: This is a work of fiction. Names, characters, places, and incidents are a product of the author's imagination. Locales and public names are sometimes used for atmospheric purposes. Any resemblance to actual people, living or dead, or to businesses, companies, events, institutions, or locales is completely coincidental.

Golden Boy / E. Davies. – 1st ed.
ISBN: 978-1-912245-39-0

# Golden Boy

# *Author's Note*

This MMMM romance features three Daddies and one very good boy (no age play). There's some mild dirty talk, exciting dirty activities, and watersports (no degradation or drinking)... the kind that can still happen when the lake's frozen. And, of course, every Twisted fairytale ends in a happily-ever-after!

## GOLDEN

"N-Nice weather, huh?"

I fumble to unzip my jacket as the stranger closes his front door with a solid thud. My fingertips are still numb from the cold outside, but my cheeks are burning under his gaze.

I finally gave in and downloaded Grindr last night. In rural Minnesota, slim pickings beat no pickings. This guy was the first one to message me, and he's spent all day toying with me, making me admit all of my secret fantasies. Then he called me a good boy and told me to come to this address at seven PM sharp.

I'm already glad I followed his orders.

He's exactly like his bathroom mirror selfie: six feet tall and broad-shouldered. He's around forty, with hints of salt-and-pepper gray in his hair. And sure, he's handsome enough. But what really drew me to his profile was the energy he's giving off right now.

Calm. Confident. In control.

This is a man who knows what he wants—and what *I* want, better than I do—and how to make it happen.

My heart is threatening to leap right out of my throat with anticipation. Despite myself, I'm still chattering to fill the silence. "Kinda cold, though. But at least it's not snowing yet—"

"You didn't come here to talk about the weather," he cuts me off firmly. Here in the Midwest, we'd call that rude... but he doesn't sound like he's trying to be mean. It's still enough to shock me into silence as he locks the door and turns to face me. "Did you?"

I stop fumbling with the zipper, my shoulders sinking. I feel the weight of his gaze grounding me until I almost forget the chaotic mess of energy and anticipation I brought to his doorstep.

"N-No," I whisper, but I hesitate and trail off. He raises an eyebrow and folds his arms, but my tongue is frozen in my mouth.

I don't know if I can bring myself to finish the sentence.

*No, Daddy.*

If I say it, I'll make it real. Here on the verge of discovering the parts of myself that I've tried to ignore, I'm suddenly realizing that there's no going back once I've started this.

But I think it's too late. I *want* to give in to my fantasies—and to the men who make them come true. I just can't stop making small talk. What I need is someone to take over...

Oh. Of course.

I need a Daddy.

Just for today, of course. But naming this stranger for what he is to me today also means putting voice to my own desires... truly owing them for the first time.

Can I do that?

He still says nothing. His gaze sweeps up and down my body, making me feel naked despite my half-zipped puffer jacket.

I've been fighting back a boner for the whole drive, but there's no stopping or hiding my body's reactions now. One look makes my cock swell, and now I'm throbbing hard in my jeans.

He's not even trying to be subtle about studying my growing hard-on, a faint smirk dancing around the corner of his lips.

That expression—and my body's reaction, the surge of heat in my belly—melts away my skittishness. I lick my lips and nod, swallowing despite my still-dry throat.

"Yes, Daddy."

I expected him to smile or praise me, but he isn't.

He's grabbing me by the hair, dragging me down the hallway to the bathroom.

As the shock gives way to white-hot pain across my scalp, I yelp. "Ow! Ow, ow, ow!" I can't stop myself from scrabbling at his hands, but he doesn't let go, forcing me to stumble along with him.

Any illusions of control have been shattered.

By the time we get to the bathroom, my chest aches. It's almost infuriating how fucking hot this is when we can both feel how empty it is, too.

This isn't an internet tab I can close or a fantasy I can forget after I blow my load. This is a real, living, breathing Daddy. He can see every blush, hear every moan… feel every tremble of arousal.

I can't lie to myself when my fantasy is staring back at me and he can see exactly how much it turns me on.

"Behave," he instructs me firmly, letting go of my hair.

I'm blinking away the stars in my eyes as he pulls my T-shirt over my head. I keep my hands on the back of my head, letting him pop open the button on my jeans and slide down the zipper.

I'm barely able to register my surroundings: pale green bathroom tiles, some shadowbox picture frame with sea shells, coordinated blue soap dispensers on the sink. Instead, I sway into him and close my eyes, giving in to the feeling of strong hands tugging against clothing.

When I open them again, he's crouching by my feet to get the last of my clothes off.

I'm totally naked, so fucking hard that my cock is almost flat against my stomach.

Daddy stands up again, grabs my hips. "Step back," he orders, locking gazes with me.

*It's happening.*

I have to trust him to steer me… in more ways than one.

I clutch the back of my head, clumsily raising a foot to clear the tub edge. Now the other foot.

*What now?*

As I raise my gaze to stare at the Daddy, he lets go of my waist and folds his arms again. "Good. Now… get down on your knees."

My jaw drops.

This is *definitely* a test, but I can't help staring at him, frozen with surprise. Are we skipping right to it? Is he actually going to…?

*Right now?*

"Now, boy."

He didn't even raise his voice, but pure instinct drives me to my knees. "Yes, Daddy," I whisper.

My toes curling with frantic excitement. From this close, I can see his crotch—and the hard line of his cock against his own jeans. I'm a bundle of nerves and horniness. I'm so close to finally living out this fantasy for the first time, and nothing he does now could really calm me down.

Daddy smiles briefly. "Good boy," he says. "You'll make a great slut, won't you?"

"Y-Yes," I squeak as he reaches for my face. I flinch, but he's just casually shoving my hair out of my eyes. He rakes it back under my hands until I'm holding it all out of my face. "I'll be a great slut," I promise breathlessly.

Anything to keep his other hand moving as he unzips himself, reaching through the fly.

Then, just inches away from my lips, he pulls out his dick. The sight is making my mouth water: thick enough to wrap all his fingers around, flushed red, with a rounded mushroom head.

But he's not fully at attention yet. Phew.

I'm transfixed by the sight of his fingers sliding to the tip and back to the base. He strokes himself slowly, spreading his feet to brace himself in front of me.

*Oh my god, it's about to happen.*

"There's only one kind of weather you came here for."

I don't know if he meant it as a joke, but I can't even giggle. I'm transfixed and trembling, my eyes glued to the tip of his perfect, thick cock. He rests his other hand on the inside of his leg, his thumb and forefinger framing the base.

*Come on come on come on...!*

I can barely breathe, I'm so taut with anticipation.

"Beg me," he orders.

Oh, fuck. "Please," I gasp.

I want so badly to reach for myself, wrap a hand around

my cock and start jerking it. But I don't think I'm allowed yet…

"Please, what?"

I whimper and close my eyes, tilting my head back. "Please use me," I gasp, too desperate to even think about what I'm saying. "Please, Daddy!"

"That's right. You just want to be used." His voice is thick and rough, like he's fighting through the last of his own resistance. "Marked. *Owned.*"

My cock jumps against my stomach, and I tremble with the self-control it takes not to reach down *right now*…

"Please," I gasp, my eyes flying open again.

One burst of heat across my chest follows another. Then it turns into a steady stream, trickling right down to my aching hard arousal, and I can't stop myself any longer. I reach down and grab my cock, jerking it hard and fast.

Daddy doesn't stop me. He just groans, leaning back and relaxing into it… but he never stops watching me.

"Oh, fuck," I moan. I feel filthy—a thousand times better than I ever dreamed I would.

This stranger is jerking himself off right in front of my eyes. He's fully hard now, but another spray hits my chest every few strokes, sending another burst of lightning-sharp pleasure straight to my core.

I'm clenching up… every muscle is taut… oh, fuck. Oh, fuck, I'm going to come so fast!

My desperate whimper is met by a grunt, a few last droplets flicking across my shoulders. Daddy groans and fucks his hips forward into his hand, slamming his cock through the ring of his fingers, getting closer until he's right in front of my face…

"Yes," he growls.

"Please," I whimper, jerking myself as fast as I possibly can. The edge is flying closer. I can't help myself, can't stop it, can barely hold back… "I'm yours, Daddy. Claim me!"

"Fuck…!"

His cock jumps in his hand, and I whimper in delight as he grabs the back of my head. I tip my face back and open my mouth, peeking through my lashes at his final few desperate thrusts.

And then he lets go with a long, low groan of ecstasy.

He's marking me, all right, aiming every drop right at my face. When some of it lands on my tongue, I make a soft sound at the strange bitter taste, but I don't flinch away.

I want it all. Everything Daddy has for me—it's all mine.

"Nnnh!" I gasp. The world is narrowing, and I really *can't* stop it anymore. "I'm… I'm almost…!"

"That's right, boy," Daddy says firmly. "Give in. Show Daddy how much you like it."

"Yes!" I throw my head back as I buck into my own hand.

The blackness takes me, and it's not going to let me go. Wave after wave of it, shaking me from head to toe, lighting up my very bones from the inside out… it's like nothing I've ever felt before.

I'm finally blinking, sluggishly coming back to life.

God knows how long I spent squirming on my knees against the hard, cold tub, but it was worth every second and then some.

"Shower head there," the stranger tells me, and I find it and rinse myself off. He hands me a towel afterward and asks if I want a glass of water, but my head is a million miles away.

"No," I mumble as he leaves me to towel off and get dressed, trying to sort through the fog in my head.

It wasn't a bad sexual encounter. Not in the slightest. I'm almost giddy from it still. What I want is exactly what I just got... but with something more, too.

Affection.

That ache in my chest lingers as I get dressed and see myself out the door, through the cold, to my still-warm car.

I've had plenty of intimacy that never came close to scratching the itch of my hidden desires. And now that I've indulged those desires, I don't think I can keep that part of me locked away any longer.

But I don't know if I can get both at once—here, or ever.

I thought coming here today and doing this for the first time would scare me, but that part turned out to be... surprisingly easy. The best I've ever had, actually. What's rattled me is another thought—one that just won't go away.

What if this is the best it gets?

# CHAPTER
## *One*

GOLDEN

"You know, Goldie… we don't *have* to decorate on December first. Just this year, we could do it on December second."

"Do my bunny ears deceive me?" I gasp, dramatically clutching a fistful of tinsel to my chest.

My festive headband wobbles dangerously as I turn to stare at my roommate, so I jam it into my golden curls again. The damn thing's always trying to fall off, but what else could I expect from a pair of giant, floppy bunny ears wrapped up in LED Christmas lights?

Needless to say, I got it from the clearance section of the dollar store. People groan about it every year, but I think it gives me an air of authority.

With this thing on, I can truly take charge of Christmas.

"What?" Ellie protests. My roommate is kneeling on the other side of the living room—and a minefield of baubles between us. She's clutching a now-empty mug of eggnog like it's her only defense.

"Did you just suggest playing hooky from Christmas?

Risking—" I dramatically toss aside the tinsel I'm holding, and it flutters slowly to the floor, "—*the wrath of Santa?*"

"No!" Ellie protests, rolling her head back against the seat of the couch. "Santa will understand if we wait 'til tomorrow, that's all."

I shake my head solemnly and tip back my head to chug the rest of my eggnog, then sigh. "Ahhh. Okay. So, Christmas hooky is only forgivable in extenuating circumstances."

"You were working 'til nine today. And I've spent the whole day on my feet!"

"I hear you," I grimace.

The coffee shop was slammed today, and our customers were even more stressed than usual. This time of year, a lot of people aren't embracing the real spirit of Christmas.

"But on the other hand…" I lean into the kitchen, pulling out the rum bottle from the bottom cupboard. "I don't think we have the right eggnog to make such a momentous decision."

Ellie sits up straight, a grin spreading over her face. "Okay, fine. You've got my attention."

"I knew it!" I triumphantly pump my fist. "Here, I'll come get your mug."

She holds it out as far as possible, while I bravely risk life and limb to get there and back. After I refill both the mugs, I set them down to spike them with the all-important rum.

"There," I tell her as I pour a splash of rum into the mug. She's looking at me with raised eyebrows, so I add another. "There?" Still the same look. I tip the bottle once more. "Okay, tell me when—"

"Okay, that's good. I *do* have to go to work tomorrow. You know, after Santa's most demented helper finally lets me go to bed."

"Awww. Thanks." I grin proudly as she snorts with laughter. "But there's one more thing."

Ellie groans. "What?"

I nudge the closest bauble with my toes, and it bumps into the next, setting off a little chain reaction as they roll treacherously across the floor. "If you wanna get your eggnog delivery, you'll have to finish sorting these by color. Or else, I dunno, cross your fingers for a passing cargo sleigh?"

Ellie laughs and flips me off. "Sneaky little fucker. I can't believe you're talking me into this."

"I know," I wink at her. "But that's how it starts. One thing leads to another, and before you know it, it's three days to Christmas and the tree is still naked."

"Oh my god. Only you, Goldie," Ellie laughs, scooping an armful of blue baubles into a cardboard box.

"Naked! Out there on the Internet for all my TikTok followers to see!" I step back to fling another handful of tinsel across the branches, then fiddle with pieces to make them look perfectly random. "You wouldn't do that to a poor, innocent little tree, would you?"

"*Little*?" Ellie laughs. "You're so full of shit."

"Maybe not little," I concede with a laugh. We got this eight-foot monster of a pine tree delivered, but it still took us both to wrestle into the living room.

"Will you cut it out?" I add to the tree, groaning as I tug the branch down. It just won't

I want a TikTok-perfect tree, but this one damn branch just keeps sticking up, however many times I tug it down. Should I just cut the damn thing off?

"I dunno. Maybe it's an exhibitionist," Ellie says with a

straight face. "Is that a branch in its foliage… or is it happy to be seen?"

"It's not—" I pull it down again, and it springs up so hard it almost smacks me in the face. "Hey!"

We both dissolve into tears of laughter as she sorts out silver, yellow, and blue decorations, and I coax the tree into behaving itself.

It'll probably take a day or two to finish decorating… but it'll be worth it in the end, because it's going to look *perfect*.

And that matters to me… a lot.

"So… what's happening for Christmas?"

I fix a smile on my face. "I'll stay here as usual." I left home at eighteen and never went back—it was better for everyone that way. This will be my sixth Christmas by myself, and I'm getting used to it.

Besides, it's the one day of the year I can indulge in my secret weird hobby without anyone judging me. There's a reason I'm obsessed with Christmas: it's the one time of year I get to shamelessly peek through other people's windows.

I love it when someone leaves the curtains open and allows the passing world to glimpse what's inside. The love and laughter, little frustrations and shared joys, huge family dinners and tables full of Christmas cookies…

"You can visit my family," Ellie offers, as always. It's sweet of her, but I've only been there once for Thanksgiving. We spent the whole trip reminding Ellie's relatives that I'm way too gay to be her boyfriend.

"No, no. I'll be fine here. Really," I insist.

"Okay. If you change your mind, just let me know."

Ellie plugs in the last strand of lights around our windows. Suddenly, the room is bathed in a warm, twinkling glow.

"It's…" I trail off, backing away from the tree for a better look. My breath catches in my suddenly tight throat.

"It's beautiful," Ellie says, finishing my sentence for me.

Every year, I cherish the moment I first see the magic of the season in my own home. The warm glowing lights in the window, or the sparkling tree, or the boughs of holly add up to something far greater.

And for a moment, the gnawing loneliness in my chest lifts, and I let myself make a wish to Santa.

This is the sixth Christmas I'm making the same wish.

*I wish for a Daddy.*

Someone to teach me what I want, and give me what I need. Someone to bake Christmas cookies with, giggling and stepping on each other's toes. Someone to stand under the mistletoe with, just gazing deeply into each other's eyes until we kiss…

"Happy with this?" Ellie asks, popping my fantasy bubble by squeezing me around the shoulders in a hug.

"Yeah," I murmur, swallowing the ache in my throat.

"You sure?"

Until I look through the right window and find the Daddy of my dreams… this will have to do.

I clear my throat and nod. "Yeah. Yeah, I am. And, Ellie…? Thanks."

Ellie shakes her head and wanders through the living room to gather our empty mugs. "You know what? This was nice. I think I needed it. Even if it was just an excuse to drink rum on a Tuesday night. So thank *you*, Golden."

She somehow looks more at peace than earlier, and I don't think it's entirely down to the rum.

"Hey, so…" I follow Ellie like a shadow as she picks up

our mugs to bring them to the sink. "Can we talk about work real quick?"

"Uh huh…"

"The boss called me into the office today. He said the assistant manager job is as good as mine in January." I wince as Ellie pauses and frowns at me. "I'm sorry. I know you wanted it."

Ellie sighs. She shakes the water off her hands and turns to me, leaning back against the sink. "That's not why I'm mad, Goldie. I'm mad because it's not what you want."

I blink at her. "Isn't it? I'll save up faster that way."

"For what?"

"My Someday Fund," I answer without even thinking about it. Ever since I moved out, I've been slowly adding to it when I can.

Ellie raises her eyebrow. "You mean your *Goldie finally goes to school for interior design* fund? The longer you stay at this damn place, the harder it'll be to leave. I just don't want to see you leave your dreams behind."

I swallow hard, staring at the floor.

She's right. I have a whole box of glossy magazines with Christmas spreads. I've been collecting them for years—from the thrift store, garage sales, you name it. I've studied them as much as I can, dreaming of what it must be like to have a show home, a photographer, and a budget.

Oh, the wonders I could create.

If I applied for school *and* got accepted, I could still fit shifts around classes. But our boss made it clear that the new assistant manager will be committed to the place full-time.

"Why don't you at least try?" Ellie says and turns away to wash up the mugs. "Send in your application. Start a side hustle instead, something you can quit when you get into school."

"Oh." I hadn't thought of that. "Like what…?" Making coffee is pretty much my only marketable skillset, and I've already getting all the shifts I can.

Ellie turns suddenly, staring over my shoulder.

"What?" I crane my neck over my shoulder before looking back at her. "Is it a white-haired Daddy popping out of the chimney with an envelope of cash?"

"No such luck," Ellie laughs.

"Then what is it?"

"Christmas! You're good at it, you like it… and you *love* inflicting it on other people," Ellie grins at me. "So do that."

Holy shit. That's a great idea—and I've never thought of it before.

"Put up an ad?"

"Christmas Bunny for hire," Ellie laughs. "No, just kidding—"

"That's it," I gasp, raising my hand to catch my sliding headband just in the nick of time. "You're a genius! I can Design and execute…" I adopt my announcement voice as I wave one hand in front of me like a giant billboard. "*Christmas.*"

I don't even need to go to school—I could practice right now!

"Goldie—"

"This is great," I breathe out, pacing furiously back and forth across the kitchen floor. "I have so many mood boards I'll never use! Oh my god, and all my Christmas ornament bookmarks—I can make recommendations! Curate them by theme! Wait, is that a thing? A Christmas curator?"

"Goldie!" Ellie laughs, and I finally look at her. "I was gonna say, help people hang their Christmas lights and stuff."

"Oh. Yeah. That makes more sense."

I mean… I've never hung lights outdoors. Like, on a ladder and everything. But how much harder can it be?

"So," I breathe out excitedly. "If we advertise tonight on like, local Facebook groups and stuff—"

"Whoa, whoa, whoa, mister," Ellie laughs as she turns off the kitchen light. "This genius is on her way to a certified bed."

"Oh, yeah," I laugh. "Right. That's fair."

Something tells me that Ellie's already done more for me than she'll ever know.

If I fill the world around me with Christmas magic, maybe… just maybe… I can start to believe there's more than enough love out there to fill my home.

And even my heart.

I've still got a hand on top of my head to keep the head-band in place as I stare into the distance. "Good night," I murmur absentmindedly. "And thanks again."

On her way to her room, Ellie stops next to me for long enough to tug one of my bunny ears. "Spread your Christmas Bunny magic, weirdo. Good night."

Oh, I will.

# *Two*

## JUDE

"COULD YOU PLEASE CAUSE *MORE* OF A DISTRACTION WITH THE ladder, dear?"

"Nye!" Star groans. "Don't say that. He'll get out his hammer."

"Mmmm. I'm listening…" Nye snickers.

I'm balanced on top of a stepstool. In one hand, I'm clutching the end of the Christmas light strand. The other is groping blindly across the ceiling beam that's currently blocking my view of my husbands.

"It's not a hammer in my pocket," I quip. "I'm just happy to see you."

After twelve years together, most of our flirting doesn't go anywhere. But it helps the three of us remember that we love each other, even—or especially—when we're annoying the crap out of each other.

"Actually, I'm not listening," Nye changes his mind. "I *have* to finish this Powerpoint today."

"Aha!" I just found the plastic clip, so I grin and snap the light strand into place. "Gotcha, you little bastard."

"And I need to focus."

"Me, too," Star chimes in pointedly.

Uh oh. We've been together so long that I can feel the twin long-suffering X-ray stare without even looking at them.

Usually, it means, *Jude! You're pacing around the room again. Take that call in the office, please.* And in the interest of marital harmony, I usually listen.

But today's ruckus can't be relocated.

We're already two days into December, and it doesn't feel right to open our chocolate advent calendar doors without mood lighting.

"You can always work in the office," I tell them, trying not to grin. I know perfectly well that their glares are hot enough to set the beam on fire now. "I have to do this."

Star groans. "*Right now?*"

"I haven't even started the outdoor lights. If I don't give you outdoor lights, my complaints box will fill up."

We're lucky enough to share the roster of husband duties three ways, but hanging the lights is firmly my job.

Nye would short-circuit the whole block if left alone with power cords. Star sometimes helps, but he can spend an hour making sure every light on a string is pointing the right way.

I wind the power cord around the beam and then hop down from the stepstool to plug it into the complex network of extension cords—meticulously planned for electrical safety, of course.

"You're right," Nye says from the couch, sighing as he looks up from his laptop. "Sorry, baby. We do love the outdoor lights. It's just..." he trails off, pinching his nose and staring at the screen.

I hate how often I see that look on his face lately, like he's stretched too thin. His usual sass is turning into snappishness a little too often. I know he feels bad afterward, but that's no easier on everyone.

"A lot of work to focus on," Star finishes Nye's thought, looking down at his screen with a sigh. He's been picking up the slack for a lot of his coworkers over Thanksgiving, and he hasn't taken time off yet.

I'm only three years older than my husbands, so I try not to give unsolicited advice too often. But now and then, I can't help myself.

"You know, we could solve a lot of problems at once," I tell them while opening the last box of indoor lights for the kitchen. "But you won't like the answer."

They both look up at me while I move the stepping stool to the last ceiling beam.

We all take turns being on the pointy end of our three-way relationship… and that isn't even a euphemism, though *that's* true, too. What I mean is, there's always someone around to take a side.

And right now, it's two against one. But that's never stopped me before.

"Take time off work, help me decorate. Get into the mood of the season."

Star narrows his eyes. "Jude—"

"You need to take more time off anyway," I cut off their protests. "You're getting into that mood again."

Nye sits bolt upright and folds his arms, clicking his tongue primly. "*What* mood?"

"*That* mood."

Star raises his eyebrows. "It's not as easy as that."

"It is, though." I don't pull the *I'm older and I know what I'm doing* card very often. But I learned early how to set boundaries and make my bosses respect me. I wish they would, too.

"Oh, really?" Star purses his lips.

It's a trap I can't help running headlong into, any more than they can stop themselves taking my bait. We all know how this argument is going to go.

"All it takes is doing what I say once in a while."

Star snaps his laptop closed and stands up. "Jupiter Behr," he snaps. "How many fucking times?"

I grunt with frustration, yanking the end of the light string out of its coil to snap into the clip. "I'm not talking out of my ass. I'm only trying to help."

"And we didn't ask for help," Star retorts. He grabs his work stuff and shoves it into his bag while Nye snaps his laptop shut, too.

Great. They're going to storm off together and bitch about me, leaving me to complain to our Great Pyrenees— and Blanche never takes sides. She just wants everyone to stop fighting.

Right on cue, Blanche whines softly from the huge, fluffy dog bed in the corner, stirring from her nap.

My frustration sits heavily but uneasily in my stomach as my husbands march for the door. I fumble with the coil of lights until I almost drop the damn thing on the floor.

"So you just wanted to complain about the noise, huh? Not look for solutions?"

That's not fair, and we all know it.

I shouldn't be taking this chance to revisit the delicate subject of work-life balance. But I can't help myself. Something in me needs to be... I don't know, listened to? Respected?

*Hell, they could pretend to humor me once in a while.*

But our relationship doesn't work that way. It never has.

Star pauses to look over his shoulder at me. "Jude. We are *not* your boys."

"Of course not. You're my Daddies," I snort with irritated amusement.

It's a running joke that we're all Daddies just waiting to be old enough to find a boy. We're all just versatile enough to make it work practically—especially in the bedroom—but none of us is really hardwired to give up control.

Star is standing there wearing a look of strained patience.

Oh. Right.

He's throwing me a bone, instead of following this argument all the way to the point where we give each other the silent treatment until dinnertime. Even Nye is holding his tongue, raising an expectant eyebrow.

*I don't deserve them sometimes.*

"I'm sorry," I sigh as I wind the strand around the beam until I reach the next clip.

But my brain is racing. What if he's serious this time?

I frown, draping the rest of the lights over the beam so I can step down from the stool. "Do you... uh, do you actually think I need one? A boy to boss around—"

"*Yes,*" they both say in unison, barely waiting for me to finish the question.

"Oh." A fluffy white bear nudges against my leg, and I instinctively reach down to scratch Blanche's ears. "Where do we, uh, find one of those?"

"I'll ask Santa," Nye says drily. "In the meantime, go look for a handyman. It'll be faster than us helping, and you won't even get electrocuted."

In fairness, that was only once... and Nye gave me a *lot* of apology blowjobs afterward. But I don't really want to repeat that experience.

I grunt, acknowledging that it's not a bad idea.

Nye clicks his tongue. "Come on, Blanche. You want to come to Stir?"

"You can get a Puppuccino while we work." Star joins in, patting his thighs.

Blanche whines excitedly, galloping across the kitchen.

"That's not fair. You're taking my emotional support bear!" I groan. "What next, the house?"

"You're hanging lights, big daddy. On ladders. You really want a freshly-napped Blanche around?" Nye smiles wryly.

Damn it. That common sense is exactly why I'm married to these two.

"Fine. Abandon me, everyone." I wave them off to the front hall. "I'll just keep hanging lights here, all alone. Or I'll find some big, masc Daddy bear on Grindr to help."

"You do that," Star snorts, stalking off to the front hall to pull out his boots.

"See you," Nye calls out, but Star is conspicuously silent.

I grunt in return, listening to the front door close. And at last, ironically, the house is silent.

I plop my ass down on a stool at the kitchen island, pulling out my phone to Google local Christmas light hanging. Somehow, I end up on Facebook instead, but that's all right.

I can waste a few minutes scrolling and finding memes to send to our group chat. Nye and Star will see them when they're done with their work days, and it'll help thaw the ice.

But then I see, in a local residents' group, a post last night. It's by a guy called Golden.

Is this a scam profile?

Ha. I'm one to talk. My parents hated me enough to name me Jupiter... and then some. Why not Golden?

He's posted a simple graphic with Christmas lights all around it. Red curly text at the top says, in all capitals, *MAKE CHRISTMAS MAGIC.*

The ad goes on to describe his Christmas light-hanging services, and then... inexplicably...

Well, there's a pair of red bunny ears at the bottom of the ad. Next to it is a phone number and a slogan: *The Christmas Bunny is here to help!*

My mouth opens and closes a few times, trying to make sense of it, but I've got nothing.

"What the hell? Who is this guy?"

I tap on his profile picture. It was taken from a distance, but I recognize the sign he's standing next to—it's a map at the local nature reserve. All I can see is a man with blond, curly hair, dressed in jeans and a plaid shirt.

I'm feeling something real weird when I look at his profile. A flutter deep in my stomach. I haven't felt that since the best day of my life: the commitment ceremony.

The argument with my husbands must be getting to me, that's all. But whether it's the universe or the terrifyingly knowledgable algorithms, someone is looking out for me.

Today of all days, I could use some Christmas magic.

My lips silently move as I type the number into Whats-App, and his profile comes up.

"Okay, Christmas Bunny. Let's see what you've got."

# *Three*

## GOLDEN

"REMEMBER, EACH NUMBER CORRESPONDS WITH THAT diagram. It goes left to right, starting with, uh… that box. I'll grab the rest as we go. Make sense?"

My jaw is hanging open, making it awfully hard to find any words at all.

I was already speechless the moment my first customer opened the door. Jude Behr is a six-foot-three, barrel-chested man, and now it turns out he's the first person I've met who does Christmas better than I do.

And that's not all.

If anyone asked me to describe the perfect Daddy… it would be Jude.

It's not just my dick doing the thinking. Sure, he's hot… five o'clock shadow grazing an angular jaw, deep blue eyes that could pierce my soul and pin me to the spot, and a musky, woody cologne that pierces the cold air and climbs into my brain…

But something else makes me want to get on my knees and do anything he asks.

It's something in Jude's presence.

Is it the way he stands, speaks, moves? The form-fitting black wool coat and cozy, knitted red scarf he's wearing? Maybe it's just pheromones, I don't know. Point is… it overwhelmed me before I even knew what was happening.

Way before I had a chance to prepare myself for it.

And now Jude's waiting for an answer.

Shit. I need to give him some kind of answer. A *yes* will do, but it doesn't seem like the right word when it's more like… *fuck yes holy shit I thought I was going to be helping little old ladies put lights around their windows and I get to decorate this gingerbread mansion for a smoking hot Daddy!*

"I'm in love."

*Shit*, not that answer!

In the chilly air, my cheeks are suddenly flushing hotter than a pizza oven. Jude's eyebrows climb into his hairline as he blinks at me.

"W-With your system! Your lights. Your Christmas." Kill me now. My mouth is moving without my say-so. The more I say, the more his lips gently curve up in an expression that isn't quite a smile, but it's certainly not mad.

Far from it.

"Your Christmas lights system," I stutter, giving him a pleading look. "It makes very sense. It's very sense—sensible."

"Good," he finally says.

Whoa.

With one simple word, he stopped my rambling just before it becomes excruciatingly embarrassing for both of us. But he waited long enough to make sure I knew what he's doing.

What does *that* mean?

He finally smiles at me, resting a hand on the diagram

taped to the top box in the pile. He pats it before stepping back into the doorway. "Very good."

A little shiver of pleasure runs down my spine at the way the syllable rolls off his tongue…

The only thing that would make it sound better is if he said "boy" after it.

Okay, *that's* my dick talking.

"This will go smoothly, won't it?"

"Yes—" Oh, shit. I cut myself off right before I add, *Daddy*. The tip of my tongue is even touching the roof of my mouth as I blush furiously, just praying he didn't notice.

We've spent all of three minutes together. It's going to be a long fucking day ahead of us if I make things awkward now.

Jude glances at the ladder leaning against the house, then looks me up and down. I try not to squirm under his gaze, but I'm regretting wearing my oldest, faded blue jeans.

They really don't show off my ass enough.

*Focus, Golden!*

"You going to be okay with everything?" Jude asks.

What? It's going to be dead easy. All I have to do is get up the ladder, attach the strand to the corner of the house, and get back down.

And not think about how tall the ladder really is.

And not get distracted by Jude.

So as long as he leaves me to it and stops giving me that smouldering hot look… I'll be just fine.

"Sure. I'll get started now." I grab the top box, carrying it down the steps. It's hard not to fumble with everything when I can feel his watchful eyes on me. Once I've put it down next to the stairs, I bend over to study the diagram, then open up the box.

As I shrug the coil of lights over one shoulder, I hear boxes sliding over the porch. I glance up, only to find Jude heading toward the ladder.

Of course! He's going to brace it while I climb.

I draw a deep breath of cold air, wincing as my nostrils stick together.

*Wow. If that didn't kill my boner, nothing will.*

"Thanks," I murmur with a nervous blush as I approach him, my palms sweating inside my winter gloves.

Without the stacks of boxes between us, there's nothing to stop the gravitational pull I'm feeling toward him. Right to my very core, every cell of me wants to be sucked into his orbit.

And I barely even know him.

What the hell is happening to me?

"It should be stable," Jude says as I desperately struggle to focus on what he's saying. "But just to make sure."

He steps back for me, holding onto the side of the ladder. Then he looks straight at me. Those blue eyes are locked on mine, like I'm the only thing in the world that matters.

Despite all my winter layers, I feel naked... and safe.

I'm only five-foot-nine, which means Jude is smiling down a good six inches as I rest a foot on the first ladder rung.

"Climb on," Jude murmurs.

Fuck. My pants are suddenly tight. Despite the chill in the air, my cock is stiffening in response to his choice of words —and every dirty fantasy they conjure up.

*Jude lying flat on his back in snowy white sheets, one huge hand wrapped around a thick cock. I'm kneeling over his lap, thighs quivering and eyes huge as I press him against me...*

"If you want to, of course."

Jude's breath appears as a puff of steam in the air, evaporating just before it can reach my cheek.

I gulp so hard that I swear my Adam's apple almost disappears. "Yep," I squeak, grabbing the ladder with both hands. I'm practically flinging myself up it now, climbing before I let myself think about it.

And… I'm at the top.

"This end goes there?" I call out, fishing out the end of the loop and looking down at Jude.

I catch my breath, expecting to freeze up… but I don't.

*Huh. Maybe I'm okay with heights.*

"That's the one."

I shuffle to the side of the ladder and hook the strand through a clip, then another. I slowly descend the ladder to follow the trail of clips, and within what seems like seconds, the strand is done.

"The ladder isn't even shaking." Jude lets go so I can feel it for myself, holding his palms up toward me as I climb down.

It makes me feel confident enough to scramble to the ground, a big grin on my face. "Yep. I'm good now."

"Great." Jude smiles at me. "I'll go inside and get the rest of the boxes. Hot chocolate?"

I blink at him. Is he asking about *my* Christmas system? "Hot chocolate…?"

His eyes crinkle with amusement. "Yes. Hot chocolate. Would you like one?"

"Oh!" I catch my breath with excitement. Daddy Jude—I mean, *Jude*—is offering me hot chocolate? "Yes, please!"

He's heading inside, and I can't believe I've managed to hold back my grin. I practically dance back to the ladder, balancing a whole stack of three boxes. How lucky did I get with my very first customer? This is going to be a piece of cake!

All I have to do is follow Jude's orders.

# CHAPTER

## *Four*

### GOLDEN

Individually, ladders and lights are easy. But together? I'm starting to realize they're a whole lot harder.

"You fucker," I groan as I reel in the strand of lights dangling from the roof.

I'm supposed to follow the roofline along from the corner of the house to the porch. But that means I can't clip the whole strand of lights in at once.

So I have to clip the strand in, hook the coil over the ladder, climb down and move it a few feet, and climb back up. I haven't even finished my third string of lights, but I'm out of breath and sweaty.

I've seen how big that diagram is.

*I'm screwed.*

I growl at the coil. I dropped it on the last trip and it unrolled all the way to the ground, and somehow when I coiled it back up, it didn't go back the same way.

I finally manage to extricate the next few feet, and while I'm clipping them in, I see the next clip. I could just lean out a little…

There!

The coil won't stay on the ladder now, so I pile it up in the gutter to climb back down again.

My feet are just touching the ground as I hear someone clearing their throat.

"Oh!" I nearly jump out of my skin, whirling about.

Jude is back. He's standing a few feet away, holding a metal Thermos in one hand… but for the first time, he's frowning. "I don't like it."

Oh, shit.

My stomach ties itself in anxious knots as I spin around to look at what I've done. "I-Is that right? I followed the numbers—"

"The design is fine," Jude tells me, his stern look never wavering. "But I don't like you leaning over."

I sigh with relief, but he's not done yet.

"I don't want you to take any risks, sweetheart."

Oh my god. The nickname rolled off his tongue so casually… I can't have heard that right.

No, I did.

He's looking at me for a reaction, his lips curved in that mysterious little half-smile. But he isn't tongue-tied and blushing like me. I guess that's what makes him the Daddy.

*Daddy Jude.*

It would fit him so well.

Okay, so I'm never allowed to say his name again, because there's a pretty big risk of a *Daddy* slipping out in front of it.

"Um… I… sorry… I won't take risks—" I stutter, crossing my fingers that he isn't *actually* mad at me.

"It's your neck on the line," Jude tells me, but not unkindly. He reaches out with the Thermos, pressing it into my hand, and then he shoves his hands into the pockets of his quilted jacket. "And mine, I guess. I don't know my insurance coverage."

It breaks the tension, making my breath rush out in a laugh.

"I'm going to go get the rest of the lights. No risky business. Or else," Jude tells me with a finger wag...

And I swear he just winked at me.

Holy shit. He's deliberately flirting with me!

I giggle louder this time, a grin spreading over my face as I set aside the Thermos. I put my hand on my heart to promise him, "None. Not even any hijinks."

When he goes inside, I let myself take a minute—and a big, deep breath of cool air—to cool off.

*No risky business.*

Riiiiight. Easier said than done.

---

Fuck.

I wanted to be better at this than I am. I mean, the part where I flirt outrageously... that's going just fine. But I don't think that's what he's paying me for, and I'm doing pretty badly at the rest of it.

I'm stuck at the top of the ladder, holding a coil of lights and fuming because I can't quite reach the next clip around the corner of the gable. At least, not without leaning... and I don't want to break Daddy's—uh, I mean, *Jude's* orders.

*I could do it anyway. Lean over really quickly, while he isn't here. I'm sure nothing will happen. He never even has to know...*

No. He gave me an order. I don't want to sneakily disobey. *I'd* know, and it wouldn't feel right.

But how can I keep going? Do I drop the coil and trust

the weight won't rip clips out? Put it in the gutter, where it seems to get tangled up straight away? I can't stay up here forever.

A professional would know what to do.

*Come on, Golden. Think.*

Oh, shit. The front door is creaking open, making me blush with embarrassment.

*Busted.*

Jude squints up at me, then sets down the boxes he's carrying next to the rest of them on the front porch. "Not even a shenanigan in sight."

All of my frustration just melts away at the easy warmth in his voice. It makes me feel like everything is going to be okay—like everything *is* okay.

"No. I behaved myself this time," I tell him as he leans over a box. He's looking at the diagram to figure out which ones to bring here next.

"Good boy."

Wait.

Holy shit. Was that wishful thinking?

No, I definitely heard that right. But it was so casual… like he knows exactly what he said, and he's giving me a minute to really squirm about it. Or else it came so naturally to him that he hasn't even realized what he just said.

Either way, it's fine with me. *More* than fine, according to the heat coursing through my veins as my blood all rushes south. But I'm still stuck on a ladder, and my downstairs brain should not be left in charge of deciding how to get down.

*Can I surreptitiously unhook this strand, move the ladder six inches over, and start again?*

I think it's been a minute or two of me staring into space,

desperately trying to stop my brain from replaying his words over and over. And it feels good. It feels fucking great, like finally reaching an itch deep down inside me somewhere.

But what feels less good is being stuck here.

"Uh oh," Jude says from the bottom of the ladder, and I stare straight ahead, my cheeks flushing with embarrassment. "Someone's in a pickle, huh?" he adds.

But he's only gently teasing me. He isn't laughing at me, and he isn't mad. So I can do it. I can look him in the eye, admit that I'm in trouble, and ask for help.

"Yeah," I tell him, clearing my throat sheepishly and looking down at him. "I'm not sure what to do."

I didn't expect him to look like... like *this*. Intense, yet calm, like he knows exactly what to do.

I shiver with anticipation, my lips slowly parting.

He puts a hand on the side of the ladder. "May I come up there?"

God. He's so considerate, asking permission—acting as if I'm not obviously out of my depth.

Letting me keep my pride.

"You can come wherever... you want..." I trail off, already blushing furiously. I bite my tongue before I can dig myself a deeper hole.

So much for pride.

A grin appears just above Jude's red scarf. I could swear that's a glint of mischief in his eyes. "I will," he answers in a deep rumble.

Like a promise.

The ladder is creaking. It shifts under me as he climbs onto the bottom rung, but that isn't the reason my heart's racing.

I have to think of unsexy things right the hell now. Whatever he's planning, I think he's about to get up close and personal with me. Certainly close enough to discover exactly how much I like being called a good boy.

Shit. No. *Unsexy* things.

*...Bad boy?*

Oh, no. The seam of my jeans is digging into my hard-on. I don't dare reach down to readjust myself, either, because Jude will see it from down below.

*He probably already sees everything.*

My dick twitches, straining against my thick outer layers as Jude climbs toward me. Closer, and closer, and—

"Stay still."

I shiver to my toes at the firm, take-charge tone in his voice. Before I can so much as say *yes, sir,* he's here to help.

Like he's arrived to be the Daddy I really want right now, when I'm fucking up so badly.

Jude's standing one rung below me, his chest pressed against my back. However weak my knees get, I can't go anywhere without his say-so. Which is great, because if I slide down the ladder now...

Well, let's just say I used to drag sticks along railings to make a *clackaclacka* sound. I'm so rock-hard that I think I'll make a sound just like that, only it'll be a hell of a lot more painful.

I press my lips together, but I can't help the snicker that escapes.

"What is it?"

"Um..." I choke on my laughter. I *definitely* can't say. "Nothing."

"Mmm," Jude hums.

The laughter disappears, because Jude's taking the bundle of lights from me. His glove brushes mine, and even with the layers between us... I swear, an electric charge is dancing along my skin like the freaking Northern Lights.

It races through my back from my shoulders to my thighs—everywhere our bodies are in contact.

Holy fuck.

I'm starting to get worried about coming in my pants. Is that actually possible? Can I come hands-free, just from having my ass nestled into a smoking-hot new Daddy's crotch?

If there's ever a moment to find out... it's *not* while we're ten feet up a ladder.

Jude shifts his weight to the other foot and effortlessly slides the strand into its clip. Then, he hooks the bundle of lights around the corner of the roof. "There."

"Oh," I whisper. It was just a few inches too far for me to reach. "Okay."

*God, why am I so bad at this?*

I'm great at making beautiful displays. But I guess this isn't really designing so much as executing. And I'm not usually on a ladder juggling everything...

Jude's voice cuts through my thoughts.

"I'm sorry. I've never had anyone else do this part. I didn't think about other people reaching it."

His every word is a warm puff of air against the back of my neck, a welcome tiny blessing in the cold. Even through the cold, I can smell his musk again, and... the way he's pressed up against me still? Oh, god. I want to find some excuse to drag this part out.

"Um," I whisper, shaking my head slowly to try to clear the fog.

Thank god I don't have to look him in those deep blue

eyes from this distance, too. I might die of excitement and horniness and embarrassment.

I gulp hard and shake my head. "It's okay. I-I'm sorry, too. I'm not very good at this. It's my first time. Outdoors, anyway."

"First times are tricky," Jude murmurs. Together with the way he's holding the ladder, his arms are kind of wrapped around me... it's kind of like he's holding me close. "Especially outdoors. Most people choose the beach, though."

A tiny squeak escapes as my cheeks burn. I want to protest that he knows what I meant... but I also don't want this to stop.

Jude laughs softly. "You're doing everything you can. That's all I can ask for."

Holy shit. This is the most romantic moment of my life. It takes all I have just to cling to the ladder as I meekly nod.

"But we really shouldn't both be up here." Jude pulls away from me to climb back down.

"Oh. Right." I bite back the wave of disappointment as I wait for him to reach the ground before following. As soon as my feet touch the ground, I slide my hands in my pockets, subtly tugging my jacket down.

Jude's already moving the ladder around the corner of the porch to get to the other side of the gable. I squint up, trying to see the distance between clips, but he holds up a hand.

"Let me do this part."

"A-Are you sure?" I stare at him, but I can't hide the relief in his face.

"Of course." He braces himself on the lowest rung, then climbs up. "Just keep passing me the next one. We'll work faster as a team," he says like it's no big deal.

My heart soars with gratitude. "Okay," I say, beaming at his retreating back.

"And remember to have your hot chocolate." He flaps a hand. "Go on. Shoo, boy. Drink up."

*Well, if Daddy says so...*

"Oh! Yes!" I rush over to grab the Thermos from the snow, cracking the seal to pour a small, steaming cup.

Wow. Okay, on top of all the other ways this man is perfect... add his hot chocolate to the list. The first sip unfolds across my tongue all sweet and smooth. Then it easily slides down my throat, warming me from the inside out.

"How is it?"

"Perfect," I murmur and tip it back to savor the last few drops.

I can't miss the way he smiles to himself at the compliment, standing a little taller on the ladder. It makes me smile to know that I can make *him* feel good, too.

If he'll let me, I want to find every wa I can ways I want to do it again—every way I want to find every way he'll let me do so.

Even though I'm the one standing on the snowy lawn, my head's firmly in the clouds.

## CHAPTER
# *Five*

JUDE

EVEN I'M SURPRISED AT HOW FAST I WORK WITH GOLDEN. HE gets my system without needing anything explained twice. When I reach for the next bundle of lights, he's ready and waiting to clamber up the ladder with it.

That isn't the only pleasure in working with him, of course.

All of his sneaky little stares are adorable. It's like he thinks being on a ladder means I can't see him looking.

It's so easy to be around this boy.

How do I know Goldie's a boy? The same way I know I'm a Daddy.

It's like a secret pulse, a shared heartbeat that goes unheard to most of the world. I'm not always right about everything—ask my husbands—but this? I'm almost never wrong.

A boy in need of a Daddy stands out like, well... a Christmas light against the snow. It helps that he stutters and trips over himself to obey even the smallest command.

Plus, I saw his Grindr profile.

It wasn't *completely* on purpose. But when I went inside on the last hot chocolate run, I checked my phone in the bathroom. I saw his smiling face pop up on the grid, and it turns out he has the simplest profile ever.

*Seeking: Daddies, watersports, love.*

One part of that took me by surprise. But it's always the sweet, innocent ones.

And it's almost unreal how sweet he is. I couldn't have imagined a better boy if I tried—especially for the mood I was in earlier today.

I want to know more about this boy. And we're so close to finishing now, working side-by-side to finish the last of the lights on the front porch.

This might be my only chance.

"So, I have a question."

Goldie perks up and smiles eagerly at me. "Yes?"

I shake my head, not even sure how to ask the question about whatever the hell I saw on his ad. "The Christmas Bunny…?"

"Oh!"

Golden's laugh until now always been a shy little chorus of bells. This time, it's a belly laugh—abrupt and loud, and enough to make me grin despite having no idea what's so funny.

He gropes in the biggest, zipped outer pocket of his jacket, pulls something on, and puts it on his head.

"What the hell?"

White, fluffy bunny ears. With…

"Are those Christmas lights?" I shake my head, almost speechless at how hideous this thing is. "Is that a—"

"A Christmas bunny!" Goldie's smile turns into a ten-megawatt grin. He's reaching behind his ear—and now the strands of LEDs around the white bunny ears are lit up. The red glow on either side of his face makes him look like some weird-ass Christmas ghost.

I kind of love it.

I have no idea why. It's awful. It definitely should never have been made, and was intended to be thrown away long ago. The ears look like they used to be fluffier, and they're more gray than white.

But the fact they're clearly often-worn and much loved makes them so much better.

I could ask a lot more questions, but I'm growing increasingly aware that our time together—at least, the time I've paid him for—is running out.

"Okay." I shake my head. "So is that your full-time job?"

"Oh! No! By day, I'm a barista," Golden tells me with a bright grin. "And sometimes evenings." Then his smile finally wavers, and he looks down. "I started doing this to earn extra money, because... well, I've always loved Christmas. But maybe I should just stick to making lattes."

"No," I murmur. "You've helped me out a lot."

"Really?" He's brightening again, biting his lip as he gives me an uncertain look. "But I'm not very good."

I smile and reach across the railing to put a hand on the back of his. "Really," I promise.

It's been a whole lot more than Christmas decorations. Or even flirting, or listening to him singing Christmas carols badly whenever I go inside.

Deep in my belly, the heat of desire—stretched out over hours—has morphed into something else.

Hope.

Goldie has helped me realize that my husbands were right. I *do* treat them like boys sometimes. And they love me, so they put up with it... but they're never going to enjoy it.

At best, telling them what to do makes them roll their eyes in fond exasperation. It certainly doesn't make them flourish the way a boy does—and they don't draw it out of me without even trying.

I don't know, but something tells me it's not just any boy who can do this for any Daddy. I know my husbands would like him. He works hard, and he's kind and bubbly and fun. They'd both think he's hot, but would he make them react the same way?

*Shit. Do Nye and Star have sides of themselves I've never gotten to see?*

For me, Goldie is...

He's kind of a lot, and I didn't expect to have to figure out what to do about it.

"Is something wrong?" Golden murmurs.

Shit. I jolt back to awareness, realizing I've still got my hand on his.

"No," I tell him quickly and pull away, clearing my throat and leaning on the railing. "No, not at all. I just... didn't expect *this* from a Facebook ad."

Okay, apparently I can't quite keep the eagerness out of my voice. So much for being the cool, calm, and collected one.

*Good job, Daddy.*

Phew. I got away with it, though, because Golden is beaming obliviously at me. "Yeah. This has been great."

"So are you going to keep going?" I ask, watching him wrap the last strand around the corner post. "Be a professional light-hanger?"

"Tada!" Golden tucks in the end of the strand with a flourish, meaning we're officially done. Then he turns to face me. "Fuck, no."

I burst out laughing.

"No, thank you, please, and never again," Golden goes on. His eyes are sparkling, his cheeks glowing. He looks radiant, and somehow that makes his displeasure even funnier.

"So what do you want to do? Is coffee your real passion?"

Golden isn't even giggling at me. He just turns to lean on the porch railing, gazing off through the trees toward our neighbor's house.

"Maybe." For the first time, he sounds… different. Sad.

My heart sinks, and I lean against the railing next to him. A shadow is flickering across his face.

I know that being able to read him so easily, even without knowing him well, is a gift. I want to be careful with it so I don't scare him. But I don't think he's going to come out and admit anything more unless I push.

And if he doesn't tell me what's wrong, I can't help. So I stay silent, waiting and hoping that he speaks up.

"I moved out the day I turned eighteen," Golden says softly. "It was all too fast to plan to go to college or anything. I've been dreaming, saving up, ever since… but I think I've gotten a little lost in the woods."

*Oh, Goldie.*

That's a lot to take in all at once, but none of it surprises me. This boy appreciates Christmas the way I do. I'd bet our reasons are the same, or near enough.

"I'm proud of you for making it through," I tell him quietly, resting a gloved hand on his shoulder.

I can't even feel his body heat through my glove and his

jacket, but I swear my hand is burning up already. I want to grab him and kiss him until that sadness lifts, and he looks all bright and optimistic again.

"Yeah?" Golden whispers. He finally sneaks a look at me.

"Coming from that place... of course you're eager to grab the first job that comes along, and the second. Maybe they aren't quite right for you, but that doesn't mean you shouldn't keep trying."

The look in his eyes fills me with a rush of emotions I never expected. It's like he's been alone in the dark for a lifetime and someone's striking a match.

*I want so much better for him.*

I choose my words carefully. "I enjoyed our day together. But I don't think this made you happy the way you'd hoped, did it?"

Golden hesitates, looking guilty, and then he hangs his head and nods. "I'm just trying to do a side hustle for my Someday Fund. I really do love Christmas. But I think I'm supposed to design, not... execute."

"I think so, too," I tell him with a soft smile. "You're obviously loyal. Don't let that get in the way of your future. Life is a buffet for hungry boys. Keep taking a bite of this, and a bite of that... keep on sampling until you find what really nourishes you. When you're well-fed, everything's better."

It's silent.

Seconds tick by, and it's still silent.

It feels like minutes are passing in the snowy evening, but it's probably only been ten or twenty seconds without saying a word. We're holding eye contact, each searching for something we can't quite name in the other.

Suddenly, Golden's eyes look wet. He doesn't quite cry.

He keeps trying to look me in the eye, pride making his jaw stiff.

*Something hurts.*

I don't say anything to embarrass him. I just hold his gaze, hold my breath, hold everything inside me back from tearing into the people who make him feel that way.

Better to hand him a shield than go rushing in with my sword and put him on the defensive.

"I don't know if that really exists," Goldie murmurs at last. He finally turns and faces me, resting his hip against the porch railing. He folds his arms tightly over his chest like he's hugging himself. "Is everything better for you now?"

*Fuck.*

I should have seen that coming.

I clear my throat and look away, biting my tongue before I can reflexively brush him off.

I don't talk about it often these days. Not many people besides Nye and Star know the truth—or almost the whole truth. But with everything Goldie just admitted, I think he already guesses.

But all afternoon, he's been nothing but honest with me— in heart, soul, and body. I think I owe him the same in return.

"It's not perfect," I have to admit. "But it's been a lot worse. A *lot* worse." I sigh softly. The last thing I want is to add the weight of my longer lifetime on top of this young man's burdens.

Golden frowns, giving me a look of sorrow and understanding. His arms unfold as he gazes up at me.

His expression—eager, waiting, listening—calms down this strange and wild, yet important part of me. It pulls me forward, making me grow up and step into who I've become, because of who Golden needs me to be.

Holy shit.

"Then I got brave enough to look for better. I found people who *do* love me better. I got married. We made up the rules and invented a weird little family of our own." I smile at him through the warmth and tightness in my chest. "I know what it's like to have people who fight *for* you, not against you."

Golden furrows his brow and looks away at last. I can see him working through everything in his head as he turns to lean on the railing again. At last, he looks up.

"So… how do you get brave enough to look for better?"

I nod slowly and glance away.

It almost surprises me how eager I am to find the right words, to speak and move carefully… to treat him well. I might never see him again, but I know this moment could stay with him forever.

Golden is this innocent, precious diamond. He's been ground up between a lot of stones all moving through his life, heading their own directions. I don't want to be another stone. I want to polish, not grind.

*Well… I want to grind, too. But that's a different matter.*

"Are you hungry?" I answer him with a question of my own.

Goldie nods so fast that I know he didn't even have to think about it. "I have been for my whole life."

"Then listen to your hunger," I tell him softly. "It knows what you need to order."

Deep down, it's not just my kind heart making me help Goldie out in a moment of uncertainty. There's a part of me that gets off on doing this—letting out the side of me that naturally takes charge and says what people need to hear.

But I don't have to hold that in check around Goldie. He's a boy—and a boy who needs what I have to offer.

I reach across the railing and grip his forearm. He sucks in a breath and slowly looks up at me, and I can't miss it either—the sharp lightning suddenly crackling between us.

If we were talking about anything else, this is when I might kiss him. Instead, I let go of my grip on his forearm and slide my hand carefully up to his shoulder, watching Golden's pupils dilate.

He sighs softly, almost inaudibly, and closes his eyes as his lips part. They look so soft, so full and warm…

*I don't want to hurt him.*

However badly I want to lean down and close the distance between us, I can't let myself do it. This has gone way past the point of no-strings-attached fun. If I kiss him now, I'm going to be promising something I just don't know if I can give.

*The first thing Golden needs is a Daddy... but the last thing he needs is a broken heart.*

I clear my throat, forcing myself to let go of him and step back. "Now, do you want to see what we did today?" I ask.

Turning to walk down the porch stairs gives me a precious few seconds. It's just enough time to put myself together and be the Daddy here, *before* Golden sees everything written on my face.

"Uh…" Golden murmurs, and then he jolts back to life. "Oh! Oh, yeah!"

"Stand on the path," I direct him. When he's scurried over there, I add, "Cover your eyes."

He groans, but obediently raises his hands to cover his eyes.

I push the plug into the socket and grin as I circle around to stand behind him, playfully sliding my hands over his. He drops his hands and folds them eagerly in front of him, bouncing on his toes with excitement.

A little flirting never hurt anyone.

"And… three, two, one…"

I slide my hands away and prop my fists on my hips, looking over the finished work.

The lights outline the roof and gables, the windows and porch, in glimmering soft white. Against the dark green of the forest to the right of our property, and the darkness of the quickly-fallen night… it's magical every time.

Even though it's familiar to me, it's nice to see it through his eyes for just a moment.

"Whoa," Golden whispers, nodding to himself. "And all the same color? Yeah, it is. Strong design choice. It could look too same-y, but the broken roofline makes it work."

*This kid just keeps on surprising me.*

I shake my head, smiling to myself as I run my hand through my hair. "Thanks. So… here you are." I step to the side, pulling out the envelope of cash to hand over to him. "Thank you for all the help today. If you want to come in to warm up, you're more than welcome."

Golden hesitates, looking at the envelope and me like he can't quite believe that I'm actually paying him. "My plea-sure," he finally murmurs and tucks it away in his pocket.

"So…" I start, but I hesitate when Golden looks at his watch and sighs.

Shit.

He has to go somewhere.

"Um..." He shifts from foot to foot, and I'm finally putting two and two together.

I've been giving him a lot of hot chocolate all evening. And he hasn't been inside, even once. I sort of assumed he was taking care of his needs somewhere outdoors... but perhaps not.

Ohhhh. How could I have forgotten his Grindr profile? He *likes* to be left squirming and desperate, doesn't he?

I thought I was getting off on this the most, but he's beaten me at my own game.

"Let me guess. You gotta go?" I say with a sly smile.

His eyes snap wide open. He blushes as red as a tomato, and I hold my chuckle inside. "Um... oh! Go. Yeah. Sorry to go so fast. But I've gotta get ready for my shift at the coffee shop."

"Oh," I frown. "Damn. Otherwise I'd invite you in for a bite to eat... or at least to warm you up. Shower you with praise for this incredible work," I gesture around the house.

Goldie blushes right to the tips of his ears, squirming on the spot. "Th-Thanks. But I had fun—I mean, this was great —thanks for hiring me, and uh, for the hot chocolate and everything!"

He doesn't try to hug me. Now that I know what game he's playing, I'd love to insist on ending with a hug—if only to keep him here and torment him that little bit longer.

But I don't think it *would* end with a hug.

"Thanks again for your help, Golden," I tell him, unable to resist giving him a knowing grin that makes his blush deepen. "See you."

"Bye...!" Golden calls, skittering across the snow to the driveway. He fumbles with his car keys, suddenly looking back like he's worried that he's offended me.

I wink and raise my hand in a wave, grinning as it works. He ducks his head and blushes, tumbling into his car and starting it up.

This boy might be young, but he knows exactly what he wants. He's a *lot*. And I've enjoyed every single moment of it.

Man, oh man. I think my husbands are right.

*Again.*

# CHAPTER
## *Six*

GOLDEN

It takes all my self-control to look at the street and not just stare at Jude in the rear-view mirror until I turn around the corner.

Have I been living just across the lake from the perfect Daddy for all this time?

My cheeks hurt from smiling. I barely know what to do with myself. Working hard to make him happy has left me with a whole new sense of satisfaction, and now that I've had a taste, I want so much more.

*So* much more.

What the hell is going on with me?

I'm twenty-three and chronically horny—this is far from the first time I've struggled to contain myself.

*So to speak.* That last flask of hot chocolate has just about pushed me into downright desperate territory.

Holy crap, did Jude really guess what I'm into? How did he know? Maybe he didn't know. The sly, knowing smile around his lips makes it impossible to tell if he was just enjoying teasing me about anything he could.

Or else he knows, and he likes it.

*What I wouldn't have given to stay and find out if he really does want to be Daddy Jude.*

I lick my lips and clutch the steering wheel as tight as I can to keep my thoughts on the road.

The fantasy can wait until I get home, and so can I… but only just.

Pushing myself to my limits feels so good, and I've never been able to explain why. All the signals of my needs get mixed up and spat out as a bone-deep ache. It's rare that I get this kind of chance to drag it out for hours—all while flirting outrageously with a hot Daddy.

But I'm not far away from the real painful kind of need, so I'd better get home and reward myself for all my patience and hard work.

It's that time of year when evening catches me by surprise, even if it isn't yet dinnertime. I'm driving slower than usual. The roads are always quiet here, but I don't want to discover any ice via sudden braking.

Something unusual flickers in my peripheral vision as I approach a stop sign.

"What…?"

I slow down for a better look.

An elderly lady is holding a lit strand of lights. She's holding onto the porch handrail with one hand, the other on the back of a wobbly wooden chair that sits at the edge of the porch.

She looks like she's about to climb up onto it.

"Oh, shit!"

*That's* why Daddy Jude paid me so generously for doing as little work as I did today. I'm supposed to pass along the goodwill.

Even in this state, I can't stop myself from helping her. I bet it'll only take a minute or two.

I turn on my four-way flashers and throw the car into park, then climb out.

"Ma'am? Can I help?"

The lady peers through the darkness at me, and then looks down at the lights in her hands. "Oh, you're so kind," she says, hesitating. "It's—it's only this one string giving me trouble…"

I'm already jogging up the driveway, waving off her thanks. I might not be a six-foot-three tower of a man like Jupiter Behr, but from the top step, I bet I can reach. "No problem! Just glad I can help."

"Thank goodness for tall young men who like to help!" I'm at the porch steps as she reaches out to shake hands. "I'm Dorothy."

"Golden. All right, I won't need that chair. Does it belong there?" I pick it up and nod toward the little matching wooden coffee table against the side of the house.

"Why, yes, it does." Dorothy stands back, still holding onto the light string. They're a mix of red, blue, green, and yellow lights, casting strange shadows against her snowy white hair.

She chatters to me about how her nephew meant to fix the chair, and he was supposed to come home, only he had some urgent work thing come up. I nod politely as I take the string and clip it in place.

I didn't grab my hat and gloves from the car, and my ears are already chilly. I'm weirdly grateful for the distraction from my most pressing concern.

"Oh, you work so fast!" Dorothy gasps as I finish clipping it in place.

I feel like a professional suddenly—and it feels surprisingly nice. "I just got finished doing a house around the corner," I tell her with a proud grin. "So this is easy. All done!"

"Well, thank you again," Dorothy tells me with a smile. glances toward her front door. "Can I bring you cookies in exchange for your help?"

I hesitate. Normally, I'd love to get homemade cookies from a sweet granny… but this isn't the moment.

I *really* have to get home now.

"That's really nice of you, but I really gotta run," I tell her with a breathless laugh, raising a hand to wave as I trot down the steps. "I just want one thing in return, Dorothy. Promise me you won't stand on that chair again."

Dorothy laughs and backs up into the doorway to escape the cold. She's still beaming like I've made her whole night. "I promise. Merry Christmas, Golden."

"Merry Christmas!" I wave goodbye and clamber into my car, starting it up to pull back onto the road.

My breathing is shallow as I drive across every bump and pothole, and the pulsating tightness in my belly is starting to turn unpleasant. But I'm surprised at how full my heart feels.

I didn't expect to feel so overwhelmed—so over-filled, in a way—with everything I'm holding right now, emotionally and physically.

I feel like I was *needed*. And I was finally in just the right place to answer the universe's call for help. It was only one silly strand of lights… but it made such a big difference.

For the first time in a long time, I feel like I can do anything I put my mind to.

# CHAPTER
## *Seven*

GOLDEN

As I rush through my front door, it feels like I'm coming home from a date. I'm breathless and bursting with uncontrollable excitement. And I'm on fire with a more intense, more exciting sexual frustration than I can remember feeling in ages.

I swear, most of the time I spent with Jude, I was trying desperately to hide my hard-on. I've been edging myself for hours, unable to do a thing about the way his silky-smooth voice wraps a spell around me.

It's almost the opposite of the Grindr date. I'm not hollow but satiated—I'm on-edge, frustrated, and overwhelmed, like I'm being showered with everything I want all at once, and it's too much.

Shit. That was not the mental analogy to go for.

"Fuck fuck fuck hold on," I pant out loud, peeling my jacket off and tossing it on the hallway floor. "Just a minute more. That's all I have to do."

Tossing my jacket on the ground, I hastily pop the button

on my jeans so I can crouch and unlace my boots. I kick them off one at a time, moaning softly as I straighten up.

"Bathroom," I gasp, and I run for it.

Ellie's at work, so I have the house to myself for a few hours before I leave for my shift.

I intend to make the most of it.

This delicious agony is the only thing I've ever found that comes close to the feeling of an orgasm.

And it makes sense. Clenching down hard, like I'm doing right now, must use some of the same muscles. It makes my cock twitch, and my body instinctually responds by getting excited, and before I know it…

I end up like I am right now—fully erect, now with *two* urgent problems.

"Come on, come on, come on," I pant.

I'm shoving the bathroom door closed, stripping without a second thought. I turn the shower water on to warm up, then wipe the sweat off my brow.

*So close.*

Fuck. Ow!

The sound of water is making it even harder to hold on. I'm clenching uncontrollably, twitching as I double over the sink.

Come on. Breathe. Just breathe through it, Golden.

I know how this works. But I hate how good it feels when it hurts. I'm so damn hard I'm not even sure I *can* let go.

If only I'd been brave enough to stay. Take Daddy Jude up on his offer, admit what I really want, let him take over…

He'd smile and kiss me and admire how cute I am when I'm whimpering and overwhelmed with need.

And then he'd solve this problem for me.

Fuck.

With him, I bet I'd get what I really want: a Daddy to look at me like I'm the most precious thing he owns, while marking me as *his* to cherish.

Jude said he's married. Maybe, just maybe, I'd be into his husband, too? And his husband would like sweet boys who desperately need to be claimed?

In my fantasies, that's how it's going to work. I'll have two men to share me. Not just two men… two *Daddies*.

"Oh, fuck," I gasp, scrambling into the shower and closing the door.

My fantasies are really running wild now.

A wave of arousal flushes through me, prickling all the way to my toes and tingling to my fingertips. I can barely breathe, barely think straight. I can't help touching myself, running my palm gently along the shaft as I imagine more than one Daddy fixing all my needy desperation.

I'm going to picture Jude's husband as a generic handsome guy right now, maybe a little bit softer. It makes sense that he'd be into someone a little different than him, and while I'm wildly fantasizing, I like the idea of a sweeter Daddy, too.

Not that I don't like the stern look on Jude's face when I'm disobedient. That does *all* kinds of things to me.

Of course, it would be Jude's hands on my shoulders, pulling me against his chest as he leans back on the tiled wall. His hands are strong and firm and warm, full of confidence but not bravado. Just the quiet, firm command that I yearn for.

"Admit it: this is where you need to be."

"Yes, Daddy…!" I moan, leaning obediently on the cold

tile wall. I grimace and close my eyes, but my body heat is already starting to warm them up—slowly. Soon, I'll be able to fool myself into thinking it's him. "Give me everything, please. I need it."

I wrap my fingers around my hard manhood, squeezing tight as I pump my hand to the base and back to the tip.

Then I lurch over, curling in on myself as those muscles deep inside clench and shudder again. I flinch and twitch, but he wouldn't let me stay there all curled up.

He'd want to see my face the whole time.

I can feel Jude's palm on my cheek, tipping my chin back to help me stand up straight.

"Please…!" I whimper. "Please, Daddy!"

Maybe it's just the dizzying heat that's making my head spin, the force of the daydreams, but… I can't hold back the long-awaited desire that's clawing its way out of me.

*I'll go back there*, I promise myself, even if this is the heat of the moment. *I'll find out if he feels like I do.*

I can't say we've never even touched each other. I remember the strength of Jude's arms around me, his chest against my back… the curve of his soft cock nestled against my ass.

But we've never kissed, never reached under each other's clothes, never dared indulge the magnetic force that draws us unstoppably toward each other.

I still know what he is.

Jude's the real kind of Daddy… the kind I yearn for with the full force of all of my want and need.

And I'm overflowing with it right now.

Another desperate throb courses through me. I lose my breath as I instinctively clench down hard, and my aching-hard cock jumps in my hand.

Then I tighten my fingers, my moan growing into a full-out cry. I'm overflowing with ecstatic *need* and *want*.

I can't hold back any longer.

A twinge, a helpless flutter, and my fight is over.

I roll my head back against the shower wall and whimper helplessly as the ebb and flow of release sweeps me away.

The pleasurable ache grows every time I yield a little more, for a little longer. It feeds that insatiable desire that keeps me pumping my hand up and down my shaft, faster and faster.

Every burst is like a tiny orgasm: a moment of relief and pure delight in losing the battle against my own body.

And all I can picture is Jude standing behind me. Just like he did on the ladder, with one strong arm around my waist, wrapping me up in his steady calm presence until I feel so utterly, perfectly safe.

He's watching me, holding me… guiding me.

"Thank you, Daddy."

My whisper is drowned out by the roar of the water, but I let my lips form the shapes anyway.

"That's right," I can practically hear Jude whispering in my ear. "Good boy."

Oh, fuck, I almost forgot he said it! And how hot it was. The warm growl in his voice, the rumble of well-practiced words, telling me that—like any good Daddy—Jude knows what he's doing.

All I have to do is… relax.

Let go and trust him.

I stroke myself harder and faster, my grip tightening on my shaft. I'm leaking precum—at least, I think it's precum.

I'm not sure, and I don't care. I'm too busy getting completely overwhelmed by the fire in my belly, frantically chasing a cliff-edge of release. The closer I get to it, the more intensely I feel it in my bones, but the further away it seems.

It's hardly ever felt *this* good by myself. In fact, I don't even think it's felt this good in my handful of hookups.

But I feel like I've stumbled into a whole new world of pleasure—and it runs deeper than I ever guessed. I thought I'd come in seconds, and instead, the plateau I'm climbing just seems to be sloping upward.

Jude's voice is warm in my ear, and his breath is hot against my neck, and his hold around my waist is tightening…

Oh, fuck.

That plateau is coming to an end.

I see the cliff-edge, and I can't stop myself. I'm burning up from head to toe, frantic with need, throwing myself with reckless abandon toward the ecstatic bliss I so desperately crave.

*I want to come. I need to come with his name on my lips... and his cock filling me up.*

All my weight rests against the tiles behind me. I roll my head back against it, my lips falling open. My knees are trembling uncontrollably.

I can't get over the mental image of him helping me satisfy more needs than I even knew I had, all at the same time. His chest against my back, his cock pushing against me...

And then splitting me open, filling me up to the brim. Pumping inside me, groaning in pleasure as I squirm and scream and melt into a helpless, horny, messy pile of goo.

*And that's not to mention his husband.*

A second Daddy, a faceless shadow watching us with a soft smile.

"Good boy. You take Daddy Jude's cock first," he tells me, all the while stroking himself. "And then I'll have my turn. We'll make you into our perfect little slut."

"Daddy!" I whimper. "Yes yes yes yes—!"

I reach back with my free hand, my nails scrabbling across tiles as if to grab the back of Jude's head. I can just about clench his hair between my fingers, putting up the tiniest and most helpless fight.

I want Jude to bite my neck, softly run his teeth along my ear, hold me against him like a helpless little fucktoy.

"I'm yours," I gasp.

"Come for us," whispers the second Daddy in front of me, gently running his hands down my thighs as Jude stretches me open with every slam of his hips. "You know you want to. That's a good boy."

No. No, there's something better than that.

"*Our* good boy."

Oh, fuck.

It feels even better this time, sweeping through my body until every muscle goes taut at once. My back arches, my balls draw tight, and my toes curl on the shower floor as I rest all my weight on the shower wall.

I can't stop it. It's coming. I'm *coming*, I'm fucking losing control again...!

*Bliss.*

Everything disappears under the waves of all-consuming, perfect, shimmering blackness.

I cry out into the steamy bathroom air, my hands scrabbling across tile and glass as I reach out for the figments of my imagination who—for just a moment—felt like they were really there.

I drop my hands hastily and curl them to my chest, letting

the hot shower water wash me clean and keep me company
on the long drop down to reality.

For just a moment longer, I can pretend.

# CHAPTER
## *Eight*
### NYE

I'M THE HUSBAND WHO ALWAYS KNOWS WHAT THE OTHERS NEED —usually before they even know they need anything.

Just as I expected, Star's mood is much better after an afternoon at the coffee shop. Plus, we stopped to walk Blanche on the way there and back. Nobody can stay grumpy while watching our enormous, fluffy daughter happily barreling through snowdrifts.

I see the glow above the trees before we even turn the final corner. I can't help sitting up straighter, glowing with anticipation.

I feel bad that Star and I were so snarky to Jude earlier. We love how much effort Jude puts into decorating every year, making our home look warm and inviting.

"Whoa," I breathe out when our house comes into view. It's glowing like a beacon in the dark, every ridge and gable lit up by strands of lights. "Is it the same as last year? Something looks different."

Star's grinning smugly. "It was cold white last year. Now it's all warm white."

"Oh yeah?" I pull into our driveway, squinting against the sudden dazzle of lights. "You like it more?"

"Much more romantic."

I laugh as I turn off the car. "Duh. Of course you like it more."

"And more importantly, it's all his doing." Star leans back in his seat to check on Blanche, and I glance in the rear-view mirror.

After three walks today, our dog is too tired out to notice we're home. She's currently upside-down, happily napping with that silly little grin on her face. When she sprawls out, she takes up the whole backseat of my little hatchback.

A little part of me wants to enjoy a peaceful moment looking at the lights from the warmth of the car before waking her up.

"Hey, wait," I reach out for Star's arm when he unbuckles, before he can get out. "Open up Grindr."

He squints at me in confusion. "You know I barely use it."

"I know, I know. Do it," I wave a hand at him.

Of the three of us, Jude probably spends the most time on the app. I dabble from time to time, but Star doesn't mind dry spells. As long as we're all intimate—and however much we've squabbled over the years, that affection never wavers.

"Mmm…" Star eyes me and scrolls through his apps until he finds Grindr. "What now?"

I pluck his phone out of his hands to open Jude's profile. Then I click the button to tap on him. "There."

"We tapped him? I don't even know what taps mean. I'm old."

I roll my eyes. "You are *not*."

"You only say that because we're the same age," Star snorts, and I lean over the console to dig an elbow in his ribs.

"Anyway, it means you'd tap that." While I'm here, I'm spying on Star's inbox. The last messages was a *year* ago. "Good lord. The cobwebs in here—" I raise his phone to my lips to blow on it. Then I pretend to sneeze.

"Shut up," Star laughs, snatching his phone back. He goes back to Jude's profile, opening up a message thread.

"Oooh." I stretch over the console to put my hands on his shoulder and rest my chin on them. "Not even gonna wait for a tap back."

Star smirks. "Fortune favors the bold."

I laugh as I watch him tap out a quick message.

*Hot daddies in your area, interested?*

"He's online!" I laugh, pointing at the green dot on Jude's profile photo. "How long before he notices we're thirty feet away?"

Star turns to peek at the front door, then looks at me.

I can't help laughing, and he joins in. It feels like we're at a sleepover, waiting for our crush to text back.

Then movement catches my eye. Jude's opening the living room window and leaning through it. He's laughing, too.

God, it looks handsome on him.

I grin and open the car door. "Yes? Can we help you?"

"Get your asses in here, nerds."

But Jude hesitates. He's frowning, like he isn't sure if that's ordering us around too much.

It makes my heart hurt.

I love Jude for being the most firm, decisive one amongst us. When important decisions need to be made, we turn to him. I never want to see him doubting who he really is.

Star is already climbing out of the car, opening the back door to unclip Blanche.

By the time we make it to the front porch, the door is

open. Jude is leaning in the doorway—taking up almost the whole frame. He's freshly-showered, wearing a thin, clingy Christmas T-shirt and jeans.

*Smouldering hot.*

I laugh as I watch Blanche barrel past Jude to the living room. "Is her dinner ready?"

Jude gives me a mildly offended look. "Of course. It's after five o'clock."

"I don't even know why I asked." I grin at him, itching to tangle my fingers in his hair and kiss him properly... but for the moment, I hold back.

Star reaches him first and practically body-slams him. He wraps his arms around Jude's waist, kissing him deeply.

I want to wolf-whistle, but it's not the right moment. They aren't just putting on a show—they're making up after their fight.

So I just watch with a soft smile, my hand rising to my chest. When everyone's getting along, it feels so much better. I'm a lot happier that way.

Whew. Goddamn, the two of them aren't done yet.

They're still feeling each other up all over in the doorway. Hands are going under shirts, and I'm not complaining about the view... but I am starting to get chilly.

I clear my throat. "Your audience would like to request a warmer seat."

Jude grunts and shuffles backward, and Star reluctantly lets go, starting to shed his outerwear.

I laugh and squeeze in, closing the door before I kiss them each in turn.

"Keep on going. I'll pay extra for a front-seat view."

Jude rolls his eyes at me, running his hand back through his hair as he makes room in the entranceway for us both to leave all the snowy outerwear here. "You two must have had a good day."

"Yeah. Did you? It looks beautiful out there."

"I did." Jude catches my eye.

Something is making me pause. What am I seeing? It's in the way he stands, the confidence radiating from him once again…

Did the decorations really help? Or did he get someone to help after all? Or… did he hop on Grindr?

I stand up straight and fold my arms, making a show of inspecting him. "Something's up with you."

Jude snorts at me and avoids my gaze. "Sure. Probably."

"Aha!" I grin triumphantly. "I want to know everything."

"Ooooh," Star breathes out, finally clueing in.

"It's nothing to talk about," Jude says in the voice that definitely means something's up.

"Ouch. Did he arrive at the destination prematurely?" I smirk, testing the waters.

Jude flushes and gives an irritated little huff. "No. He just helped with the lights, that's all."

"But you wanted him to help with other things," I persist, following him right to the kitchen. He starts to make hot chocolate, and I hop on the counter to watch.

"See? I'm serious about finding you a boy," Star chimes in, leaning thoughtfully on the counter.

Jude sighs and drops the defensiveness for a moment. "No. If I want fun, I can find that."

I wink at him. "Oh, big man. Mr. Popular."

He flips me off. "I mean… right now, that's not it. I want…"

"You want more than fun?" Star lights up, showing off exactly why we give him that nickname. "Does this mean group dates? Are we finally getting the boy of our dreams?"

Jude's face says *yes*, but his body language says *no*. He folds his arms, working his jaw around as the microwave whirs. "I think I've used up a lifetime of luck just to find you two."

He's watching us now with something soft and uncertain in his eyes—something that thrills me, but Star's about to leap out of his skin with excitement.

I think Jude will freak out if Star goes into full excited puppy mode, so I scoot over to put a hand on Jude's folded arms. "We love you, too. And I'm sure the boy of our dreams will come along sooner or later."

"You really think so?" Jude frowns at us and unfolds his arms, and each of us reach out to take one of his hands.

"Whatever's meant to be will be," Star says softly.

I wink at Jude. "We'll see what Santa brings."

Then there's a moment of silence as we listen to the microwave and the Christmas carols playing over the sound system, and the racing hearts fluttering quickly into a fast-approaching unknown.

Jude's the first one to break the silence.

"Anal beads?"

I burst out laughing. "Okay, Santa's listening." I elbow Star, who I would bet a large amount of money hasn't bought either of us gifts yet.

He flushes and clears his throat. "Santa *is* listening, yes."

"Now, come on. Hot chocolate to go?" I squeeze their hands and let go as Star and Jude stare at me. "We need a tree."

If some Christmas is good for us all… more is better.

# CHAPTER
## *Nine*

### GOLDEN

I'M GLAD I QUIT THE CHRISTMAS LIGHT SIDE HUSTLE WHILE I was ahead. I took down my ad the same night I got home from Jude's place—after the hottest shower of my life, and before my coffee shop shift.

A few days have gone by, and I haven't heard from Daddy Jude. The temptation to message him is stronger every day, but despite my promises to myself in the heat of the moment...

I'm not brave enough to show up on his doorstep, in case he closes the door in my face. And if I send him a message, that's basically the same thing.

Since he hasn't messaged me, either, I'm trying to assume the worst.

*He just hired me to hang lights, and the flirting was a bonus.*

To make matters worse, I wanted to stay busy and distracted... but the only thing keeping me busy is the coffee shop.

I just finished up another early-morning shift, and I'm parked in front of the shop. I've been idly tapping at my phone while I wait for the windscreen fog to clear so I can head home.

My side hustle? Right now, it's looking more like a side coma.

The Christmas Bunny has been reinvented as a gift-wrapping service. I was so proud of myself for thinking of another idea and advertising it far and wide before I realized it's the second week of December already. I'm probably too late.

Ellie snorted with laughter when I said that and told me to keep Christmas Eve free, but I haven't even gotten a nibble.

Unless... wait!

There's a notification on my screen. It's from Whats-App... and I've only used it for my ad.

"Holy shit!" I tap the screen so fast the damn phone freezes, and I tilt my head back and groan. "Come on, phone... stop edging me! Come on. Come on, show me! Show me show me show me—"

It's finally unlocked, and I'm eagerly scanning the message.

*Hello, Golden! Are you available to help with gift-wrapping today?*

It was sent five minutes ago!

*Yes, I am :) Would you like help right now, or later tonight?*

The little dots bounce on my screen right away, telling me that my second customer is typing.

I tap on his profile, crossing my fingers. After all, what are the odds that my second customer would be an equally sweet, generous, take-charge Daddy?

Wait. The guy's name is staring me in the face, and I can't believe what I'm seeing.

Nye Behr.

Like… Jupiter Behr?

It can't be a coincidence.

I shouldn't get my hopes up, but it's too late. My hopes are already crashing through the roof of my car, floating away like a rogue helium balloon.

Maybe Jude told his husband about me, and now the two of them want to meet me…

My heart is pounding as my phone buzzes, and I scan the message.

*ASAP, please! I'll pay a rush fee for the last-minute notice… and provide unlimited cookies. :)*

I message him back right away to confirm, biting my lip with excitement as I wait for the most important message of all.

His address.

My phone is buzzing again.

And I recognize the address that I think will be burned into my brain forever.

341 Lakeview Drive.

"Holy shit," I breathe out, leaning back in my seat to rub my chest. "It's them."

Operation Please Be My Second Daddy is in progress.

---

By the time I pull into the Behrs' driveway, I'm trembling with nerves. I didn't even bother stopping by home first, because I wanted to get here as fast as possible.

I don't recognize the little red hatchback in their driveway.

"It's his husband," I breathe out, a grin spreading across

my face. I park on the road again and climb out, beaming as I approach the familiar house.

This time, I'm going to be inside.

It's snowed since last week, covering all my footprints. It looks pretty in the daytime, but I bet it looks even better at night with the lights glowing through a soft blanket of snowflakes.

I stride up the driveway as fast as I dare, but before I can even knock on the door, it opens.

"Welcome!"

Nye is only an inch taller than me and willowy... but he has this look about him that takes me aback. It's like soft velvet over steel. Somehow, I know deep down that his warm, gentle smile and soft-spoken voice hides a surprising strength that's more than just physical.

It's something older and wiser and calmer than me.

*Holy shit. He's a Daddy, too.*

A blush is already rising in my cheeks. Nye's presence is nothing like Jude's, but it's having the same goddamn effect on me.

I hoped for this, but I never expected it.

"Hi. I'm Nye," he greets me and reaches out to shake hands.

I take his hand before I say anything.

Shit. That was a mistake.

An electric shock is running through me, adding to the heat in my belly. My heart is pounding so hard I can barely hear my own thoughts. His fingers are lean and delicate, but they squeeze mine so firmly that my knees wobble.

I can barely hear myself think over my pounding heart.

Nye finally lets go, and I desperately try to remember how to speak out loud.

"Uh. Hi. I-I'm… Golden?" I trail off.

*Do I say it's nice to be back? Do I ask about Jude? Or do I play it dumb?*

Nye's eyebrows are creeping up. A teasing smile appears on his lips. "Are you sure?"

My cheeks flush even deeper red as I giggle sheepishly. "Yeah."

"You don't sound sure." His eyes sparkle as he steps to the side to let me in. "And the unlimited cookies offer only applies to this—" he glances at his phone screen, "—Golden boy."

"That's me!" I eagerly nod, looking up from unzipping my jacket. "I'm your Golden boy."

*Oh my god.*

I can't believe I just said that.

I'm praying to melt into a puddle on the floor, but it isn't happening. So instead, I focus on my jacket like it's the trickiest thing I've done in my life. After that come my shoes, one at a time.

And now I'm out of excuses.

I look slowly up at Nye, and my cheeks turn beet-red all over again. His deep brown eyes are sparkling with amusement. He doesn't even need to say a word about it.

We both know what I just did.

"Well, I'm glad for that." Nye winks at me and turns away, walking into the house.

In the game of good Daddy, bad Daddy, he'd definitely be the good Daddy. I'm so thankful I could drop to my knees and…

Whoa, nope.

I'm focusing with all I have on the open-plan house, and admiring the Christmas decor. This must all be Jude's work.

But as much as I want to ask... if Jude *didn't* tell him about me, it would get weird.

And the last thing I want to do is ruin my chance to get to know the other Behr of the house.

*Is Jude home?*

I'm half-expecting him to be in the background some-where, lurking and watching us with that quiet, commanding smile.

But I think we're alone.

"So it's just the two of us," Nye says, like he's reading my thoughts, and I stumble to a halt and stare.

They have a huge dining table... and it's covered in toys. I can't even see the tabletop underneath them all. There's dolls, board games, science kits, art kits. You name it... there's five of them in sight.

"Holy shit. How many kids do you have? Oh my god I'm sorry—"

What the hell, brain? I really should have thought before I spoke.

My hand is firmly clasped over my mouth, but Nye is laughing so hard he has to lean against the kitchen counter.

When he catches his breath, he shakes his head. "These are from my office. We had a toy drive for Christmas."

"Oh, my god. Duh." I cover my face with both hands. "We'd better get started before I open my big mouth again."

Nye grins. "Don't worry. You're Golden, boy." He waits for me to groan—even if I'm choking back a flush of arousal at the same time—before laughing. "We have a long day ahead of us. The more you open your mouth, the more I'll enjoy your company."

So much for unsexy thoughts.

My head is spinning all over again with dizzying hope as

I sink into a chair by the table and grab the closest roll of gift wrap.

I don't know how I'm going to survive another whole day of flirting.

*Very, very happily.*

# CHAPTER

## *Ten*

### GOLDEN

I can't stop freaking out.

Jude already blew my mind once. Finding out that his husband is a sexy, kindhearted Daddy too? It's almost too much to handle.

My dynamic with Nye is obviously different. Unlike Jude, he doesn't meet me head-on with that raw, masculine self-assurance. But he isn't a shy, quiet little thing either. I can see how he stands toe-to-toe with Jude when need be.

They're like, the fucking definition of a power couple.

"Hot chocolate?" Nye asks, and I light up. *More* of that delicious elixir? "It's not as good as my husband's, but we'll have to cope."

Hopefully my face doesn't say *I already know Jude's hot chocolate is great.* "Oh, that's okay," I laugh nervously. "I'd love some. Thanks."

The Nerf gun I'm trying to wrap is a weird shape. Why won't this damn paper just stretch a little bit—

*Riiiip.*

Shit. I've never been great at wrapping gifts. I usually just shove them in gift bags with lots of tissue paper and bows. I just didn't want to turn down a chance to meet Jude's husband.

*But what's the point in meeting him if he thinks I'm an idiot?*

"Oh, let's try that one again," Nye says. He squeezes my shoulder and leans over me to set the mug on the table. Then he plucks the half-wrapped toy out of my hands, slides the paper off, and grabs the roll. "Pass me a piece of tape?"

He works almost as fast as I can pass him tape, folding the edges over and taping up the ends.

"Wow. You're good. I'm… uh…"

My cheeks burn as I look at my stack of gifts. Pretty much every one I've wrapped so far, I've either ripped the paper or folded it wrong, leaving ugly creases all over. I'm trying to cover the worst parts with bows and ribbons.

"Helping me," Nye tells me with a sweet smile. He puts a hand on my arm. "And I really appreciate it."

My brain is buzzing again. The touch seems to vibrate straight down my arm and down the center of my body, straight to my cock.

Jesus.

"Uhh…" I breathe out, swallowing hard. I can't even remember what I was saying a moment ago.

Right. That I'm not good at this.

"I, uh… I really appreciate you hiring me and I'll work hard to help you however I can." The words are tumbling out of my mouth at a mile a minute. How do I turn them off?

Nye settles in a chair next to me and picks up a cardboard box with a picture of an art kit on it. "Let's start with these. So, what brings you to offer Christmas help? Besides…" he waves at my floppy white ears, which I already turned on before I got through the door.

"My Christmas Bunny alter-ego?" I laugh. "That's pretty much it. I just really like Christmas. And I wanted to make some money—my real job is at the coffee shop by the main road."

Nye lights up. "Oh! We were just there the other day!"

"You were?"

"Yeah. We've worked there before. Star likes to get an espresso to go, when he has to go to town."

"Oh," I nod, like I know who that is. "Hopefully I get to make you coffee one morning."

Then I pause, my lips parted, as my gaze creeps up to Nye's face.

As flirting goes, that was *bold*.

Nye's giving me this long, teasing look without saying anything. He finally reaches out for tape, and I blush even harder when our fingers brush together.

"It's a deal," Nye murmurs when the present is done. "Now, we'll do one each."

Before I know it, I've copied him—one fold at a time—and I've even managed to wrap the box without any disasters.

Oh my God. He's teaching me how to be better… without even saying a word about how badly I was doing.

*That's* the kind of Daddy he is.

And as much as I want the Daddy who takes charge, I feel cared for—seen, in a different way. From the inside out.

We've almost finished the whole pile of gifts, but my eyes have just landed on one that's different from every other box here.

It looks like…

Well, it looks like a ring box. Jewelry, at the very least. None of the other boxes here looked like that.

*But aren't they already husbands?*

"Oh! I'll take that, thank you, darling." Before I know it, Nye slips the box out of my hand and tucks it into his pocket.

"Yeah. Sure." I squint at it. Now that I think about it, he doesn't wear a wedding ring. "Can I ask?"

"You can always ask. If you're prepared for the consequences." Nye winks at me to soften his words, but the warning is clear.

I hesitate and look at him closely. There's something airy and distant about him now, like he's finding his own gentle way to shut down the conversation.

Something scares him.

And that knowledge makes me just brave enough to plunge ahead. "Let's say I am."

Nye hesitates, biting his lip as he looks away through the kitchen window. I've only been here for a few hours, but I haven't seen him look like this—defensive, uncertain… perhaps even insecure.

Finally, he reaches for one of the last few boxes and starts wrapping it quickly, like he's trying to distract himself. "So, my husbands and I can't get legally married."

Wait.

Did he just say…

"Husbands?" I echo weakly. I want to be sure I heard that right.

"Yeah. Jude and Star and me. For obvious reasons," Nye rolls his eyes and laughs, "we can't get legally married. We had a little commitment ceremony twelve years ago. Just us and a few close friends. There were never rings."

*Star is their husband. There's three of them.*

"Three Daddies?"

"Yeah." Nye laughs. "It works for us. Mostly because we…" he looks at me suddenly, and creases of amusement appear around his eyes. "We find boys sometimes. But we know who we go home with."

I'm almost speechless. Even in my fantasies, there were only two of them. A third Daddy? And all of them might be into me?

*They could all bring me home.*

My jaw is still hanging open.

Nye smiles to himself and picks up the last teddy bear, turning it over in his hands. "We talked about getting rings after that. Star didn't want it to feel like we were just trying to mimic the couples out there. And Jude…"

"Yeah?" I ask, a little too quickly.

Nye didn't notice. He's staring into the distance with a frown. "He keeps up his walls. He pretends to be so grumpy, disillusioned. But that's not who he really is."

Then he pauses, his eyes flying wide open as he slowly looks at me.

Shit.

Has he figured it out? What if Jude told him my name and now he's figured out that I'm low-key stalking their house and I'm already trying to figure out how to meet Star…?

But Nye is smiling now, soft and thoughtful. He finishes wrapping the teddy bear and folds his hands on the table. "Huh. I think I figured it out. Thank you, Golden."

I blink a few times, but however long I wait, he isn't following up. "Okay," I finally chuckle. "Glad I could help. With… everything."

Nye smiles at me and rises to his feet as he puts his hand on mine. "You really have."

I quiver and look up at him, tilting my face up.

From here, he looks *perfect*. Commanding isn't quite the word. Dominant isn't, either. But he's absolutely in charge—and I know if I challenge him, he'll find five subtle ways to twist the power dynamic back to where it belonged before I even notice.

More than anything, I wish he'd kiss me.

But he lets go of my hand and heads for the kitchen, coming back with an envelope of cash. "Here you go," he winks.

I don't dare open the envelope until I get home. I have the feeling he's tipped me as generously as Daddy Jude did the first time, and it'll probably make me cry.

"Thank you," I whisper.

He rests a hand on the top of my head with such casual affection that I want to melt. "Thank you, Golden. It's been a pleasure having you."

Not as much pleasure as it could be if he *had* me.

But he's giving me that warm, certain smile that makes it impossible for my tongue to work right.

"Me too," is all I can manage in a squeak as I rise to my feet and Nye steers me to the door. "Th-Thank you good night merry Christmas…!"

I grab my jacket and flee before I can even put it on.

"And you… Golden boy."

I flee to my car with the sound of Nye's gentle chuckle still warming me from head to toe.

There's only one thing I know for sure: I'm coming back to this house. I've met two of them, and I can't stop now. I *have* to meet this mysterious Star, the third and final Daddy in the relationship.

I just need a good excuse to get me in the door.

# CHAPTER
## *Eleven*

### NYE

Santa knew what he was doing when he made sure that boy landed in my lap tonight.

"Nnnh," I groan as I slap the lid on the frying pan again, leaning back against the counter. That mental image is *not* helping all the pent-up energy that's coiling up in my muscles. "Come on, Nye. Focus on cooking."

Burning the house down isn't very romantic.

I only have minutes before my husbands get home. I'm making dinner—it's only pasta, but with carefully sliced veggies and artistic use of Parmesan, it'll look beautiful in the shallow bowls on a fully-set table.

Hopefully it'll be okay, for such a special occasion.

Nerves clench around my stomach again, and I have to stop and take a deep breath as I touch the ring box in my pocket. I don't often feel self-doubt, but it's gnawing away at me now.

Is this really the right moment to do it?

I'm caught up in the teeth of my oldest, most forgotten desire—a way of being that's so natural, it might as well be breathing. The minute Golden walked in, those sweet, innocent green eyes woke him up again: Daddy Nye.

I'm reeling from the possibilities, the *capabilities* I'm remembering within myself. Without even knowing it, Golden made me say the answer out loud.

*He pretends to be grumpy... but that's not really who he is.*

It's not just Jude.

It's me.

I've never totally lost touch with the Daddy part of me. It stirs all the time, when Star and Jude need it. But they never need me the way a real boy would—and Golden did, this afternoon.

And it's not just Jude who needs a boy... it's all three of us.

When we decided to get married—legally or not, it never mattered to us—we knew our relationship would never be straightforward. We even talked about finding a boy one day.

I don't know when we stopped taking it so seriously, when it became a running joke... but I think I know who's responsible for that.

Me.

I think I'm the one who retreated first.

I was so afraid of the three of us not being a complete unit—so afraid of what it would mean if I couldn't somehow provide *everything* the other men need—that I retreated into sass and snark. It's what I do anyway, but I started to use it to paper over the cracks instead of point out the things that need to be addressed.

I have to believe.

"Dinner was incredible," Star tells me as he finally sets down his fork, reaching over the table to touch my hand. "Thank you, Nye."

I knew he'd love the romantic touch—the candles in the center of the dining table, the soft Christmas music in the background.

Jude grunts his agreement into a glass of sparkling water. "Real good."

"What now?" Star says, craning his neck to look at the pile of gifts by the door. "Do we want to bring those to the community center?"

"We should go soon," Jude agrees.

I've spent all dinner expecting them to spot my nervous excitement and realize something is up... but they can be pretty oblivious.

I could take this chance to back down—to hide the ring box away again and save it for another day. Or another Christmas, or another decade...

Except... no. I can't.

I have to do this now.

"Wait." They both turn to look at me and I clear my throat, catching Jude's gaze first and then Star's. "I have something to say."

"Oh, shit. We'll brace ourselves." Star's trying to joke, but the look in his eye is worried.

Jude grips his water glass between two hands, and I almost expect it to shatter. "What's wrong?"

"It's not... it's not wrong," I quickly reassure them both, reaching over the table to take one hand each. "The opposite."

My husbands trade sheepish smiles as they both sigh with relief.

"I-I've been hesitating about this for a while. I still kind of am," I admit with a little laugh. "But… all I have to do is remember how it feels to be Daddy Nye again."

Jude sits up a little straighter. I'm half-expecting him to be grumpy about me challenging him, but he's not. There's a spark of excitement in his eyes, in fact. "Yeah…? Go on," he tells me softly.

Not long ago, I would have heard that as an order and instinctively twisted myself in knots to dodge it midair.

Instead, I'm hearing it for the invitation it really is—the *welcome back* to that part of me that I've been holding back from all of us.

Mama Behr is back.

"I have something for us all," I tell them with a smile as I get to my feet.

Holy shit, I'm really doing this.

Walking around the table… standing between them… sinking to one knee. Digging out the ring box.

"Twelve years ago this Christmas, we got married. We did it in front of our closest friends, because they have longer memories and higher expectations than any law in the land."

I'm almost afraid of looking up at them, but I do it anyway.

"Things have been tough lately. But I wanted to show off… *us*, at last."

Jude's staring at me with that look of awe and pride, while Star is grinning like he's fit to burst with excitement.

*Of course. That's why I married them.*

I crack open the ring box and hold it up, glancing between them.

Three thin rings are nestled inside, lined up one in a row. They're all made of beaten metal—perfectly smooth inside, but looking imperfect and rough outside. I thought that was appropriate for the three of us.

They're a matching set in gold, silver, and rose gold. Inside the bands, spanning the width of all three rings, are letters. *JNS*, for our names, and then a heart. Broken apart, they won't make sense—but together, they're perfect.

"D-Do you like them?"

The only thing in the world that could still make me nervous is my husbands' reactions. I want them to love them, not think it's a dumb idea.

But Jude is smiling softly at me. "Yeah. I had no idea you were planning this, Nye."

"It's—it's a beautiful idea." Star is holding back tears, but only just. He reaches out to squeeze my hand. "Thank you."

"Yeah," Jude whispers. "Thank you."

I clear my throat and beam at them, plucking out the rings and setting aside the box. "I thought gold for you, Jude... silver for me... and rose gold for Star?"

"Yeah..." Star trails off, his eyes sparkling as he takes the ring. "But, um... Nye?"

"Yeah?"

There's a moment of silence before Jude clears his throat. "Did you get them resized?"

*Did I...?*

"Fuuuuck."

Star bursts out laughing as I sink to my other knee. "They're too small for me. Here, try yours—"

"Same," Jude says. "Nye?"

"I'm busy languishing," I groan from the floor.

"Come on, give us your hand," Jude taps my shoulder until I raise my left hand, offering it up. Jude tries to slide a ring onto my finger, but I can feel how big it is.

"They don't fit any of us." I slowly tip forward to rest my head against the table leg, but Jude scoots forward and my head bumps against his leg instead.

"Come on," Star murmurs, grabbing me to lift me up into his lap.

I bury my face in his shoulder. "It was supposed to be a surprise for Christmas! No way will anyone get all three of these done before Christmas!"

Jude strokes my hair softly, but it's Star's words that make us all go still.

"Maybe… they aren't meant for us right now."

Jude is blushing, staring across the room like he's trying to solve a Rubik's Cube. Even Star looks startled at himself, frowning down at the ring box. And I don't need to ask the next question out loud, because it's obvious we're all thinking it.

Does that mean we have to wait… or are they supposed to be for someone else?

# CHAPTER
## *Twelve*

### GOLDEN

I've finally found something that I'm good at.

After days of talking Ellie's ear off about the Daddies I've met, and the one I haven't—and refusing to give her the address so she can meddle—she came up with the best idea ever.

Don't get me wrong, I protested at first.

"Dog walking? I don't know anything about dogs!" I said when she printed off flyers to leave in the coffee shop. But she's adamant that she's met this Star before on early-morning shifts, and she swears he usually has a dog in town.

It was a crazy idea, but I'm obsessed with the idea of meeting the third and final Daddy.

Ellie's been giving away the flier to everyone she can, and I already have four happy customers. I'm not complaining—not only do I love walking the dogs, but I quickly realized how neatly it dovetails with my *other* obsession.

Picking up and dropping off the dogs is also an excuse to glimpse so many different homes. And it fires me up so much that I'm starting to wonder if Ellie is right about school, too.

But there's one big problem: Sterling Behr, the third and final Daddy, still isn't calling me.

"Oh, hello, dear!" Dorothy pushes open the door and beams at me as I step up onto the front porch with her little terrier, Alice. "I did some baking while you were out walking… if you're interested, of course."

"Thank you," I laugh, stepping inside. I crouch down to let Alice off her lead. "I'm very interested."

"I was hoping you'd say that!" Dorothy bustles off to the kitchen, and I follow her. "There's only so many cookies I can foist on the neighbors. Would you fill up Alice's dish? There's a dear."

"Mmhmm." I grab the food canister and crouch by the dish, holding up a finger to make the terrier sit before I fill it up and let her at it.

Wait.

I swear I just heard Dorothy say *the Behrs*.

"—three young fellows. When they moved in, I thought it would get easier! Bless him, Nye just keeps sending cookies back. By now, it's practically a competition to out-cookie each other—"

"Behr?" I breathe out. "Sorry. You mean Nye Behr?"

"Yes! You know them, too?" Dorothy beams at me. Before I can say anything, she raises her hand. "Oh, of course! They have that fluffy white polar bear of a dog, Blanche. Star's always said how much he wants a reliable dog walker. I bet they all love having a handsome young thing like you around," she winks.

My cheeks are burning up. "I… uh… I don't really know Star, actually," I stutter.

"Well, that's no problem." Dorothy dusts the flour off her hands, shoves the cookie tin at me, and picks up the landline. "But you'd better hurry over there."

"Wait, what?"

Dorothy pauses before dialing to explain. "Star usually takes Blanche out at this time of night. If you head on over there, you can join him. I'll call and tell them you're on the way."

My jaw drops. "A-Are you sure? I mean, uh… thank you!"

"I'm quite sure. Now, hurry!" Dorothy flaps her hands at me and I sprint out the door, cookies and all.

There's no time to lose.

---

I'm pulling up by the Behrs' driveway, where a man is waiting with a fluffy white dog.

There's no time to linger nervously in my car or get myself together. All I can do is tumble out, my cheeks glowing with excitement and adrenaline. "I made it!"

"You did."

I stumble to a halt in front of Star and blush, suddenly tongue-tied by those words—and how drop-dead gorgeous he is.

In contrast to my chaotic frenzy of anxiety and excitement, he's smiling warmly but perfectly calmly at me. He's got a strong jawline, his hair cut short up to his temples and a little longer on top. His eyes are the most beautiful soft gray. He's a couple of inches shorter than Jude, and he looks almost as strong.

He doesn't have the mischievous glint in his eye that Nye does. Nor does he hold himself with that firmly detached command like Jude. His eyes are thoughtful and soft, and he's watching me like he knows a secret.

*And maybe he does.*

"I'm Sterling Behr. Just call me Star," he tells me, reaching out a gloved hand to shake. I take it, and my knees feel weak. "And this is Blanche."

"Hi, beautiful!" I beam as I crouch in front of her. She lurches up to me and slobbers across my cheek. It's like hugging a cloud, and it makes both of us laugh as she pants happily. I look up at Star with a grin. "Golden Girls?"

Star looks impressed. "You know your history," he tells me.

"Of course. It matters." I straighten up and wipe my cheeks, hoping I look at all graceful still—maybe even cute.

"And speaking of... I'm assuming you're that Golden boy Dorothy just called about."

"Oh, yes! Sorry. That's me," I breathe out, straightening up.

*Boy.* I could almost whimper. It's almost too much when I'm already dying of curiosity, wondering if Jude or Nye mentioned me. I can hardly believe I'm finally meeting him— the third and final Daddy.

If Star knows about me, he doesn't let on.

"I won't lie," Star says, gesturing for me to follow him along the sidewalk toward the trails. "I'm hoping you're the dog-walker of my dreams."

"I'd like to be!" I burst out eagerly. "I mean, uh..." I'm blushing already, I can feel it. "I hope so, too. It would be great."

The older man pauses and looks me up and down with a playful glint in his eye. "It would be great for everyone, I'm sure. Now, how about you take Blanche's leash, and you both follow my lead?"

"I'd love to," I breathe out. God, that was a little bit more intense than I meant to sound, but I can't help speaking my real mind.

Maybe I should wait more than ten seconds after meeting the guy, though.

Star gives me a playful sideways glance, but he doesn't say anything as he passes me the leash. Our hands brush together, and a shiver of delight runs down my spine.

It feels an awful lot like a Christmas miracle come early.

***

I think I've been doing a good job acting normal on the walk so far. Apart from pulling out my Christmas Bunny ears and adding them on top of my hat, of course—for visibility in the dark. Safety first.

Star does a good job of setting me at ease, but I still can't help being nervous. With the other two Daddies, we had more to do—more distractions mean more time spent flirting and teasing, rather than in serious conversation.

Tonight, there's a lot of silence to fill.

I've already told him about my job and this side-hustle— though I've carefully omitted the last two attempts. And somehow, I've found myself telling him what my Someday Fund was supposed to be for.

"So you want to be an interior designer?" Star looks curious. "That's a great job. What's stopping you going back to school right now?"

I bite my lip. "Well... I missed the deadline to start in January."

"When is it?"

"Uhh... probably October or November?" Star raises his eyebrow at me and I blush. "I-I'm not sure."

"Pull out your phone," he tells me.

I yank my gloves off so fast I almost drop them. After shoving them in my back pocket, I slide my phone out and look at him.

"Now what?" I ask. The *Daddy* at the end is silent, but I think we both hear it, because he's smiling in this soft, knowing way at me.

"Google it."

"Google what—oh!" I tap at the screen and bite my lip, waiting for it to go through.

And then I stare.

The regular deadline is over. But they'll accept late applications until midnight on December 24th.

Tomorrow.

"Surprised?"

I look quickly up at Star, my cheeks flushed. He isn't shoulder-surfing—he's just interpreting my face correctly. "Um... yes," I admit softly. It's kind of embarrassing, actually. "I can't believe I didn't think to at least check."

"That's why I'm here," Star tells me with a little shrug and a wink. "I believe everything that happens is meant to be."

"Especially at this time of year," I murmur, pocketing my phone. I rub my hands together, and he stops and reaches out to take my hands between his.

They're warm, even with his gloves on.

I can barely breathe. The gravitational pull of my body towards his... it's almost impossible to ignore. It takes everything I have to look up at him from just inches away, with my hands tucked safe and sound between his.

*Is this enough? Should I be making more happen? Maybe I should try to kiss him...*

There's a sharp tug on my wrist.

"Shit!" I stumble sideways, grabbing hold of the leash and finding my footing again.

"Blanche!" Star scolds her, and the dog woofs like she's apologizing. He laughs breathlessly, setting off at a quick pace again.

We definitely aren't about to talk about *that* moment that never was.

"So, what are you doing for Christmas?"

I flinch, but I try to ward off the bad vibes with a shrug. "I've always been alone for Christmas. That's fine with me."

"Mmm," Star hums.

In the silence, broken only by the squeaking of our footsteps, it's hard to ignore the unsettled flip-flopping of my stomach

Shit.

Now that I say it out loud, it sounds a lot like I'm trying to convince myself. Maybe I'm not that okay with it, after all... but I've never had a choice.

I need to take risks to get what I want from the buffet of life.

I take a deep breath and look over at him. "Maybe I'm not as okay as I pretend... but I guess I've just been waiting for my Christmas miracle."

Star smiles, taking my arm to stop me in my tracks again. He points up at the tops of the trees.

I squint and follow the direction he's pointing.

The moon is just peeking out above the snow-dusted treetops. It hangs huge and full over us, illuminating the path like it's broad daylight.

"Whoa," I breathe out.

"All things are possible," Star promises me. He rests a gentle hand in the middle of my back, but this time as he looks down at me, I don't try to lean in.

*It's not the right moment.*

"In fact... I have an idea," Star continues. "If you don't have any plans tomorrow, would you like to come over and join me and my husbands? We'd like to be Daddies together on Christmas Eve. And we'd love to walk Blanche together. It would... er... help us see if you're a good fit."

His eyes are gleaming like he knows a secret that nobody else does... but I think I've got a pretty good idea what it is.

"I'd love to," I tell him. We trade smiles, and we're off walking again.

At last, I'm feeling like I'm exactly where I'm supposed to be. And maybe, if Christmas magic is real... I'll even be *theirs*.

# CHAPTER
## *Thirteen*

### STAR

By the time I burst back into the house, the excitement still hasn't faded.

"You can praise my genius now or later," I announce, sweeping into the living room. "Which will it be?"

Nye straightens up from checking the oven in the open-plan kitchen, leaning over the counter island. "I'll gladly praise your genius anytime, darling. But don't keep us in suspense."

Jude mutes the terrible Christmas movie that's playing. Then he side-eyes it and turns it off instead, and I snort with amusement.

He thinks I don't notice him watching all the romantic parts.

"We're going to have company tomorrow night."

Both of them just blink at me. They don't seem mad about it or anything… just confused. A few seconds have already gone by, and nobody's saying anything.

"On Christmas Eve?" Jude finally asks. "*You're* inviting anyone over?"

"Yeah…?"

Nye gives me a wry smile. "Another board game Christmas?"

"Ahhh," I groan, as it hits me. "Shit."

Four years ago, I invited some friends over from for board games and booze. It quickly turned out that they'd expected us to provide a whole selection of boys and the kind of night where car keys get put in bowls.

They ended up partying way too loud, crashing on the couch overnight, and not leaving for their own family Christmas gatherings until well after noon.

I was more upset than anyone about the missed opportunity for a quiet, romantic evening with just the three of us— and that's what we've done ever since then.

"This isn't that," I insist. "It's just one person."

"Oh?" Jude asks. He stands up slowly, wandering toward me to kiss me hello.

"A boy."

Jude hesitates and pulls back instead, leaning on the dining room table. "Oh."

*Damn it. He promised to keep an open mind.*

I can see the guard going up in Jude's eyes already. I sigh, appealing to Nye for help with a look. "He doesn't have family in the area. He'll be alone on Christmas otherwise."

"Okay," Nye gives us a soft smile without even a joke about me rescuing strays and waifs.

"Are we sure?" Jude hesitates. He isn't protesting, but he's still frowning at the idea. "I just think… Christmas Eve means a lot to you, Star. You don't want to rush into anything and mess it up."

When my instincts are this loud, I'm willing to fight just a little bit dirty.

"Years ago, if we hadn't found each other... that would have been one of us."

I mean Jude, and we all know it.

He flinches, looking me in the eye for a moment before he frowns and looks away. "And let me guess: he's your type."

"*And* yours. Both of yours," I tell him, beaming at Nye. "Trust me."

"I do," Jude says quickly. "Just... don't move too fast, all right? Give him a chance to get used to... us."

"To three Daddies?" I shrug. "He knows. Or... I think he knows."

"No. To *us*." Jude pulls away from us and starts turning out the lights, getting ready for bed. "Individually, and together."

Nye huffs and stalks across the living room to grab the newspaper. "I hope you aren't implying I have an excess of personality." Then he turns on his heel to sweep past us for the stairs, gathering momentum and indignant force as he goes. "I don't think anyone ought to get *used* to us. The boy can come over. But enthusiastically on board or nothing at all—*those* are the terms."

Then he storms upstairs.

I swap looks with Jude, who raises his shoulders helplessly.

Well, shit. We both know Nye isn't really mad—he's afraid of something. At least when Jude's scared, he just acts grumpy about it. He doesn't wall me out and then light fireworks around all the walls.

"Nye," Jude calls out to stop him. "I didn't mean it as a bad thing. You make up everything we lack." He tries to press a hand dramatically to his forehead, but it just comes off as clunky.

I can't help a laugh. Jude's playing along, hoping that will soften Nye's mood.

It doesn't seem to be working.

"That can't be true." Nye spins around at the top of the stairs to look Jude up and down. "There is *nothing* lacking in you." Then he looks pointedly at Jude's crotch and sighs, sweeping into the bathroom.

"Thanks?" Jude mutters, and I crack up as I follow after both of them. "Hey, Star? How do I make this end in sex?"

Nye sniffs like he's trying to resist being amused by him. He turns on his toothbrush to furiously scrub his teeth clean.

"I think you were screwed the moment you asked that. Or... *not* screwed," I tell him, scooting into the bathroom to join the others. "But I still have a chance, so I'll let you watch us from the chair."

Nye rinses out his mouth and strides up to me, grabbing the back of my head to haul me in. I grapple for the back of his shirt, trying to hold onto him as his mouth slams into mine and sparks fly.

It's quick, hot, deep—and then it's over.

Nye makes his dramatic exit for the bedroom, and I sigh as I look back at Jude. He just gives me the *I know* look.

We're both taking our time getting ready for bed, but there's no delaying the inevitable forever. As we gaze off contemplatively in our different directions, moving through our familiar routine, we can only hope that Nye is cooling off.

I follow Jude to the bedroom, and then I pause in the doorway to watch for a moment.

Nye has settled in with the crossword on the right side of the bed. He's tapping his pen against the page, but he's staring through the paper like he's lost in thought.

Jude gingerly approaches the bed, lifting the covers. He scoots into the middle like he's worried that Nye will read him for filth.

Instead, Nye reaches out seemingly unconsciously to Jude, his hand palm-down. And just as he has thousands of times, Jude takes it between both of his hands, squeezing softly until Nye's shoulders settle down and he breathes a little easier.

It makes my heart happy every single time I see the visible signs of our fond, well-worn, yet sturdy love. And it's my turn to join the dance—in this bed, this life, this place that fits me perfectly.

I close the door behind me and join both men, taking the left side of the bed. I sleep like a log, so I don't budge when Judge climbs over me in the night.

This *is* pretty perfect. Almost enough to make me hesitate about adding anyone else.

Maybe I am pushing them too hard. Maybe it's more my hope than my gut instinct that's telling me to introduce Golden to our dynamic and see what happens. Maybe I should be listening and slowing down more.

If Golden stays, where would he fit?

*Right where he's meant to*, my heart says. And I hope to God I can trust it.

"Fine," Jude says abruptly, looking at me.

I raise my eyebrows, waiting until he bothers using his sentences.

"Fine—we can meet him to walk Blanche. And maybe even invite him for dinner. But…" he trails off, then sighs as he lets go of Nye's hand to draw the covers up to his shoul-ders. "Just take it easy on us all."

*On me*, he means.

I look up from Jude to find Nye watching him, then me. He gives me a wistful smile, and I nod slowly.

Jude has always thought he wouldn't get luckier than he already has.

It's the most romantic, sweetest, and saddest thing I've ever heard. It makes me smile to think how much he values us and the shape of the life we've built together, but at the same time, my heart hurts at what I know he believes.

He can't see that there's room in our life for a boy—someone who brings out the best in us all. There are parts of us that get itches we just can't help each other scratch. The best we can do is wait for the storms to pass.

I've always believed that love keeps its heart soft, and when Jude says things like that, they're only to protect the part of his heart that he barely ever shows off anymore.

*Our poor love.*

"And you?" I ask Nye. "You're in?"

He pauses and sucks the end of the pen for a moment.

Huh. I wasn't expecting him to think so hard about it. Nye is the heart of our home—in a lot of ways, the most sociable. He loves meeting new friends, welcoming new faces in… I thought he'd be on board right away.

Then he takes a deep breath and nods, like he's finishing a conversation I can't even guess at. "Okay," he smiles at me. "Let's see what happens."

I breathe out a sigh of relief.

We're all in this together… even if we don't know what *this* will be.

"Thank you," I tell them both, leaning over to kiss Jude. I wave a hand at Nye despite his little scoffing noises until he gives in and leans in to join us in one of those rare, awkward, nose-bumping three-way kisses.

We're all laughing as we pull apart again, turning off lights and settling under the covers.

"Good night," I murmur into the quiet darkness, smiling at the sound of my husbands' voices in return.

Jude might be the brains of the operation, and Nye is definitely the heart… but I've always been the soul, because I have enough faith for all three of us.

*And perhaps one more.*

"ARE YOU *SURE* YOU DON'T WANT TO COME WITH ME?" ELLIE calls out, running into the kitchen.

I fold my arms suspiciously as I follow. As usual, she's rushing around the house, packing totally random items into bags before she rushes out the door for her Christmas Eve family visit.

"Yes. And that egg separator doesn't want to, either." I grab it from her bag as she rolls her eyes and huffs at me. Wait. I'm looking in the bag now, and… I'm pretty sure that's our sea salt grinder.

Yeah, it is.

"Really?" I hold it up. "They don't have sea salt in Illinois?"

Ellie groans at me. "I *need* it for my special secret cookies, and I don't know if they'll have *enough*—"

"Okay, okay," I laugh, raising my hands. "I would have gotten you sea salt for Christmas if I'd known what a valuable commodity it was."

She snorts at me. "Smartass."

We exchanged gifts last night, and I'm glad she liked the

antique coffee pot I found for her. In return, she got me a bunch of craft supplies—a notebook, pens, and glue. She said it's so that I can finally cut out all the pictures from those magazines and make my own inspiration book for when I get to school.

I might have cried a little.

I haven't yet told her about the application deadline being tonight. Just in case I don't get in… or in case I lose my nerve and don't apply.

"I love you too," I tell her with a grin, catching my Christmas Bunny headband as it slides back down.

"I swear, I was going to get you something to fix that," she points at my headband with a long-handled spoon. "And yes, I *do* need this, so hands off." She drops it in the bag and zips it up before I can rummage any more. "Bring this to the door?"

I pretend to grunt and groan under the weight of it as I carry it to the front hallway, and she laughs at me.

"But seriously," she says, looking up as she crouches to tie her shoes. "You're really happy to stay and… walk one of your dogs?"

"Me? Oh, yeah." A grin spreads across my face. "It just depends whose dog it is."

Ellie pauses and looks up at me. Then she gasps and almost topples over. "Holy shit! No way."

"Yeah way."

"*Dude!*" Ellie scrambles to her feet and punches my arm. "I would have gift-wrapped you and dropped you off on their freaking doorstep if you'd just told me earlier!"

I'm not sure she's exaggerating.

"That's kinda why I didn't," I smile sheepishly at her, trying not to look as nervous as I feel.

Ellie's laughter fades away. She's looking at me for a long moment, her eyes flickering between mine. "Oh. Wow. Okay," she says at last. "This… this is a big deal for you, isn't it?"

I bite my lip as heat rises to my cheeks, but I don't want to deny the truth. "I think it might be. They're—they're real Daddies. I think they might even be the Daddies I've always wanted."

It's huge, saying it out loud. It makes my head spin.

Ellie shrugs on her jacket and smiles at me, all genuine and not even a little bit teasing. "I'm glad, Goldie. You've been changing lately. Looking more like yourself."

"Yeah," I murmur, and we smile at each other for a minute. Then I wave her off. "So you better hit the road. I've got stuff to do. Shoo. Go enjoy your bunny-free Christmas."

"You, too." Ellie grabs me for a hug. "Go make sure those Daddies enjoy a bunny-full Christmas. All three of them. Stuffing the Christmas Bunny full of—"

"Okay, okay, scram!" I laugh, picking up her last bag to hand it to her as I open the door.

She grins and winks. "And tell me everything later."

"I will," I promise. "Merry Christmas, Ellie."

I stay in the doorway to wave. As Ellie backs down the driveway, my phone starts to ring, and I spare it a glance.

Oh. It's my boss.

"Huh?" I mumble, answering it and raising it to my ear. "Hello?"

The hubbub in the background crackles on the line, telling me the coffee shop is slammed right now. "Hi, Goldie," says my boss, sounding rushed. "Listen, we could use your help right now." Then the line goes muffled and I can hear him talking to a customer.

*Aha. He's on the cash register.*

The guy barely knows how to use the credit card machine, but he always tries to schedule too few people to work and jump in instead. It never goes well. That's why he needs an assistant manager like Ellie—someone who will solve the core problems, not slap a Band-Aid on the symptoms.

I already know my answer. "I'm sorry. I can't tonight."

I hear my boss talking to someone, telling them to take over the line, and then the noise fades a little, like he's stepped into the office. "Goldie, my assistant manager needs to be available on-call. It's part of the job."

"You're right. And I'm not the right person for that job," I tell him. "Thank you for offering it to me. But everyone knows it shouldn't be me."

He hesitates. "Are you sure?" I can hear it in his voice. Ellie is strong-willed and hard-working. What scares him is the fact that she's always been perfectly happy to tell it like it is.

*But we've all got to face our fears sooner or later.*

"Yeah. And Ellie just left town for the night, too." I feel a little bit bad for my coworkers in this last hour before we close for Christmas. I might as well throw him a bone. "But she always leaves the cash register manual in the basket under the counter."

He sighs with relief. "Basket under the counter. Okay. And..." he hesitates. "It's Ellie, isn't it?"

"Yep. It always has been."

He sighs. "Yeah. You're right. Merry Christmas, Goldie."

"Merry Christmas," I tell him, hanging up and pocketing my phone.

Finally, I'm alone with my dreams.

It's going to take a huge amount of self-control not to just spend the whole day in my room jerking off to my fantasies.

*Kneeling below them all as they smile down at me, cup my cheeks and stroke my hair lovingly, stroke their cocks right in front of my eyes.*

*Jude praising me for being such a good boy. Nye correcting him, teasing me: a good little slut. Star adding the most important word of all.*

Our *good little slut.*

I bite my lip hard as I open my laptop.

There are other dreams I have to chase first. If I want Daddies like these… I have to be brave enough to become the boy they deserve.

The deadline for late admissions is tonight. I've started this application three or four times before, so I already have most of my documents together… but I always hit a wall when I got to the personal essay discussing why I want to study interior design.

*Because I like looking through people's windows at Christmas?*

Yeah. I used to imagine stuffy men in suits laughing at my application and throwing it in the trash. But now I feel something I thought I'd forgotten long ago.

Hope.

<br>

"*If given this opportunity…* wait. That's another extra space!" I swear my eyes are crossing as I squint at my application. "Okay. *I don't just want to find…*" I lean closer to my screen. "Is that how you spell peace? It must be. I have to stop second-guessing myself."

I'm exhausted despite all the coffee, but I'm so close to the end.

I'm starting over again, my lips silently moving as I read.

*If given this opportunity to study interior design, I don't just want to find the peace and joy I've always been looking for on the other side of the window. I want to learn how to walk through the door and create opportunities for connection.*

I bite my lip.

"Opportunities for connection?" I whisper, and then I shake my head. It sounds so corporate. I'm not thinking about PR stunts right now—I'm thinking about the feeling of walking into the Behrs' house, knowing that at last, I've found somewhere I belong.

I suck my breath in, and type quickly.

*—and create places where everyone can feel like they belong.*

"That's it," I whisper. A chill runs down my spine as a grin spreads over my face. "That's it!"

I was able to copy the basic stuff from my previous half-finished applications. But this time, I went all-out and told them everything: the Christmas Bunny, my family, the last few years of obsessively collecting every Christmas design magazine I could find…

Well, *almost* everything is in there. I might have left out a few details about the last month. Point is, I finally realized what I need to do.

I need to stop looking in from the outside, trying to find joy… and start putting myself in the room to *make* it.

"Okay, what time is—"

Shit. Wait. I thought I was making good time on my application… but it's almost nine PM.

I was supposed to be at the Behrs' house an hour ago.

"Oh, fuck. Fuck fuck fuck."

Shit, I can't even text Star and apologize. I guess I could message Jude or Nye... but I don't even know if they knew I was coming. If they don't... well, I was hoping that I could show up and bat my lashes.

If I break the news over messages, I look a little bit like a demented stalker. Because I guess I *have* been a little bit stalkerish... but not without everyone's consent, I swear.

*Is it too late?*

I stare at my screen, blinking back the tears of disappointment in myself. However many times I read the words, they don't change. They're washing over me like a mantra as I try to hold myself together.

*Application confirmed!*

Hm. Star said everything happens for a reason. And if he hadn't made me face my fear... I might have thought I was too late to chase my dream. Now I have proof, right in front of my eyes.

There's always hope.

The tightness eases in my throat. I scrub my cheeks and draw a deep breath, frowning at my computer once more before closing it.

Should I apologize? Will they forgive me? Did I screw everything up forever? I have no idea... but I've always followed my instincts.

And, if they're really my Daddies... the Behrs will know what to do.

# CHAPTER
## *Fifteen*
### GOLDEN

The Behrs aren't home.

Or, if they are, they aren't answering the door.

"Shiiit."

Three pairs of bootprints—and one set of paw prints—lead off the porch and across the lawn to the sidewalk.

I don't like my chances of tracking them like some mountain man. It's started to snow again. The falling flakes settle on my neck and shoulders before slowly melting into droplets of cold water on my bare skin.

I didn't bring a hat and gloves, either. If I try to chase them down, I'll freeze before I find them—*if* I pick the right trail to find them.

I should probably just leave… but I'm not going to.

*This is my opportunity.*

Most of the houses don't have fences between their front and back yards. There's no point when people could just get to the backyard via boat in the summer, or on foot in the winter. So it's easy to trot down the porch steps, circle around the side of the house, and step onto the deck.

I can feel the lake looming behind me in the darkness. All I see is snow swirling across the surface on the shoreline, barely lit by the outdoor lights. Beyond that, pinpricks glow in the distance from houses on the other side. In the daylight and good weather, I bet I could see my own little house squeezed in between its sprawling neighbors.

But it's what lies ahead that fascinates me—not that vast, cold emptiness behind.

"Wow," I whisper as I peer into the living room through the huge sliding glass doors.

The overhead lights are off, but the whole room is aglow with light. The Christmas tree is eight feet tall and lit by warm white lights, just like the exterior of the house. It's decorated in tasteful red and white baubles, gingerbread and ceramic ornaments, with neatly wrapped presents underneath.

There's a whole table full of tin foil-wrapped pans. I can't see into the kitchen, but I'd bet anything that I can smell turkey—with all the trimmings. The dining table is closest to the doors, covered in a white tablecloth. They even have candlesticks and bouquets of red and white flowers. I can't quite make out the tableware, but it looks like their finest china and silverware.

Wait.

The table is set with four places.

My throat tightens as I press my nose up against the cold glass, holding my breath so I can better see inside.

*Was that place supposed to be mine? And... is it still mine?*

Before I can catch myself, I'm tugging at the sliding door...

And it glides open.

Warm air rushes out, welcoming me with all the subtler scents that got lost in the freezing chill of the air.

*Ginger. Mulled spice. And I swear that must be Jude's hot chocolate... but I shouldn't let all the heat out...*

Somewhere nearby, Christmas carols are playing gently over a speaker system. But it's the irresistible glow of the lights drawing me inside, like a moth to flame.

I step inside and close the door.

"H-Hello?" I call out, my heart leaping into my throat. I'm sure Blanche would be barking already if she were home, and I don't see any signs of their presence.

Nobody answers.

This really is a dream come true.

All three of the Daddies know me now, but I still feel a bit guilty about sneaking around their house. I should probably go before they get back. I just want to stay long enough to drink in enough of the warmth and love that permeates every inch of this house.

Long enough to imagine what it would be like to be *theirs*.

Three handsome, kind men—each of them a Daddy in his own right, each sure of himself and able to meet some need of mine that I can't even quite describe.

Yeah. I could happily belong to them.

As I pad softly around the living room, my gaze is drawn to the staircase. The bannister is wrapped with evergreen boughs adorned in twinkling lights, leading my eye upstairs.

Their bedroom must be upstairs.

I've never been further than the kitchen and dining room. And I'm already here, right?

Just one look couldn't hurt.

**CHAPTER**

*Sixteen*

STAR

It's been a strange Christmas Eve.

I spent all day overflowing with excitement just waiting to introduce this new boy to my husbands. When eight PM came around, I started to worry and fidget and make apologies for him.

By eight-thirty, it was time to go.

Nye and Jude reassured me that they aren't mad at me, or even at the boy I invited over, but they keep giving me these worried little glances. Blanche tried her best to lighten the mood, but we all seem to have a lot on our minds.

The snowy walk was quiet. Too quiet.

It should have been perfectly peaceful and romantic with just the three of us, like it's always been. But for the first time… it doesn't feel like enough.

Stepping back onto the front porch is a relief—bringing with it the promise of Christmas dinner, good conversation, and bad movies until the small hours.

"This always feels like the beginning of Christmas," Jude says behind me. It's impossible to miss the strain in his voice, like he's forcing himself to be as perky as he can. "Getting home after this walk."

Nye hums in agreement, but I'm too lost in thought to do more than nod as I let us inside.

As usual, Blanche waits until she's in the hallway to shake herself off, but I can't muster up more than a half-hearted chuckle.

I'm worried about Golden.

I've been trying to figure out how we can track him down. I don't have his address—or even his phone number. I don't want to bother Dorothy on Christmas Eve, or make her worry that her new walker has disappeared.

"Star."

The tone in Nye's voice makes me pause and look at him, partway through hanging my jacket up in the hall.

Blanche is standing in the middle of the hallway, furiously wagging her tail. She's got a scuffed black boot in her mouth.

*I know whose shoes those are.*

Nye points at the living room, where the other boot is sitting on the back door mat. Right next to the floor-to-ceiling glass doors… which I think I left unlocked.

Without a word, we spring into action. Nye ducks his head into the guest bathroom and checks around the living room. I open the door to the garage and basement, checking to make sure the lights are off.

But it's Jude who pads straight upstairs, and then turns to look at me from the doorway of our bedroom. I glance at Nye, and both of us rush upstairs after him.

And there he is.

Half-curled in the middle of the huge bed, golden curls

splayed over the white pillowcase, hands curled up and tucked by his chest.

Golden looks precious and innocent—and, in the huge bed, so small.

"It's him," I whisper, resting a hand on each of my husbands' shoulders. "Golden."

"*Him?*" Jude whispers, looking at me like he just got hit by lightning. "He was my Christmas light helper."

Nye's jaw slowly drops. "And my gift drive helper."

We all trade stares, and then we look back at the boy who's asleep on the bed. "So?" I ask hesitantly, my heart flip-flopping in my chest.

"Santa came early," Nye whispers.

"Give him a break. He's been pent-up," Jude murmurs with a crooked smile, and Nye chokes back a laugh.

I don't believe in coincidences… and I know Golden is here for a reason. I'm the one who says what we're all thinking.

"It's our very own Christmas miracle."

# CHAPTER

## Seventeen

### GOLDEN

There's no mistaking the smell of Jude's hot chocolate. It's coming from really close by. And something warm and furry is wriggling against my leg…

"Oh, shit!" My heart leaps into my throat. I sit bolt upright, blinking sleep out of my eyes.

I'm not alone.

Jude is sitting next to me on the bed, a mug of hot chocolate cradled in his hands. He's watching me, but I can't quite read his expression. Nye and Star are here, too, sitting on the end of the bed. At least they're both smiling with amusement.

I just want to die of embarrassment.

"Shiiiiit." I bury my face in my hands.

I only meant to lie on the bed for a minute. But as soon as I closed my eyes, I couldn't keep myself from daydreaming about being tucked into bed between all three Daddies…

And I must have dozed off.

If I didn't screw it up already, I sure have now. Why didn't I just wait outside for them to come back like a normal person? And why won't the bed open up and swallow me whole?

Blanche whines, wriggling happily against me.

"It took all three of us to confiscate your boots from her," Jude informs me. I'm only praying the glimmer in his eyes is amusement. "There might still be some tooth marks."

My cheeks are burning to high heavens.

"I'm so sorry," I breathe out, my voice cracking with mortification. "I-I'll leave right now. I didn't mean to be weird, I promise, I just—"

Jude's holding out the mug of hot chocolate.

I break off my rambling and look at it, then him. He raises an eyebrow at me, still not saying a word.

He's… he's offering it to me.

My hands tremble as I take the warm mug between both palms. I glance between the three Daddies, and it only makes me lose whatever power of speech I might have briefly had.

I stare down at the rich drink and the tiny marshmallows bobbing around the surface. Then, I slowly raise the mug to my lips for a tiny sip.

God, that's good.

Perfectly silky-smooth, sweet, with just a tiny hint of a kick…

"What's in this?" I ask, frowning at the mug.

And just like that, I'm realizing that I made the right decision about the coffee shop job. Ellie would be able to tell what spice that is without even thinking twice about it. But my future isn't in hot beverages.

"Nothing illicit," says Nye with a wink. "Just borderline immoral."

I laugh breathlessly, then gulp down some more and press my cheek up against the hot mug.

"My hot chocolate mix is a trade secret," Jude says, his chest swelling with pride. "You like it?"

"Yeah. It's so good."

Blanche wriggles her way down the bed with a series of happy whines that make us all break into laughter for a moment.

"Yes. You're a good girl, too," Star tells her, grinning as he reaches out to scratch her belly. Then he looks at me and raises an eyebrow, smiling at me. "And we still have room for one good boy… if you're interested. Right, guys?"

"Mmhmm," Nye hums.

I gulp hard, my cheeks blazing hot. "Really? Even though I found my way into…?" I helplessly gesture around at the bedroom. The embarrassment is still scorching me down to my bones.

Jude's hand brushes mine as he takes the mug from me before it can slosh over the edge. I catch my breath, my lips parting. Jude doesn't say anything yet, and neither do the others.

He just puts the mug down on the bedside table, then turns back to me and takes my hand in one of his big palms. His fingers slide between mine, separating them so much it's almost painful… but it feels so good.

I can barely breathe.

All I can do is stare up at him and try to cling to the wave washing over me. Everywhere he touches me, my skin is on fire. I might as well be glowing. Not just like a Christmas light, either. Like a whole damn sun.

Jude rests his other hand on top of mine, holding my gaze with his own as he studies me for something I can't quite identify. Then, he looks at Nye and Star, but I can't read the looks they're trading with each other.

All I can do is wait for his decision.

He looks back at me. His eyes are still hard to read, but at last, a smile touches the corners of his lips. He scoots closer to me on the bed, gently cupping my cheeks in his hands and tilting my head back gently.

I close my eyes, my lips parting unconsciously as he leans down toward me.

"You found your way home."

Then he presses his warm lips against mine for one long, slow kiss as my heart bursts with joy.

This is the kind of happiness I've only ever watched and imagined from afar... and it's so much better than I ever dreamed of.

---

Everything I've tried in the Behr house is delicious.

Needless to say, I've never had a Christmas dinner like this. Growing up, I might as well have been an orphan during the holidays. My foster parents were rarely home, and the few years they were, the food looked good but was terrible. Too hot, too cold, too burnt, you name it. Waiting to get yelled at and called names... it wasn't great for my appetite.

After moving out, I got used to treating Christmas like any other day. Sometimes I'd try to get a festive freezer meal or something, but I've never learned how to cook so many things—let alone cook them so well.

I'm full to bursting, and not just literally.

My heart feels like it might explode with one more soft smile or flirtatious wink. The Daddies have made me the center of attention all evening, wining and dining me. With three of them... it's even better than I dreamed.

I feel like royalty in some fairy tale come true.

The Daddies are all happy, too. Jude gets to boss me around a little bit and enjoy watching me rush to obey the slightest order. Nye gets someone to join him in the kitchen and whisper snarky commentary. And Star gets someone who blushes and stutters happily at the slightest hint of romantic attention.

Outside, the wind has picked up, turning this evening from a romantic snowy night into an all-out snowstorm. But it's perfectly warm and cozy in the living room, sipping glasses of wine as we giggle our way through a game of Truth or Dare.

Nye is next to me on the couch, and Star and Jude are in the armchairs just across from us, making a perfect little circle.

The game's going well so far. Star had to lick the roasting pan, Jude had to do his best Irish jig, and Nye has just finished describing his most embarrassing photo—a Polaroid that he says doesn't exist anymore, of him with moustaches doodled all over his face at a college party.

It's my turn.

But I have another idea. "I think I should get to ask you all—collectively—a truth or dare."

I catch my Christmas Bunny ears, shoving them into my hair. I twist my curls around them to try to keep them in place. And, if I'm honest, because I'm nervous about what they'll say.

They exchange looks—amused at first, and then something more complicated. It looks like they're having an argument without even saying a word. At last, Jude sighs and speaks for them all. "Okay. Truth."

Something tells me that he was outvoted.

And I'm glad. Beneath the silly high-school antics, I think we can all feel the serious conversation that needs to happen—and soon.

"Have you ever done something like... like *this* before?" I ask, waving at myself and them.

"Not seriously," Jude says, looking at the others as they shake their heads. They're all watching me.

For the first time, they actually look a little bit nervous... and my chest relaxes with such relief that I sag back into the couch.

Don't get me wrong—I love that they're confident, self-assured Daddies. But I need them to be real, too. If I wanted to be here for just the night, I'd be okay with them being flawless, cartoon character Daddies... but I want more.

I wanted to see *this*. Their fears and worries, too, not just their confidence and smooth charms.

Suddenly, it feels like there's room for me.

"Really?" I murmur, biting my lip with excitement.

Jude nods. "Together or on our own... it's always just been fun."

I set my wine glass down carefully, my cheeks heating up as I glance at them through my lashes. "And this isn't fun?"

Star opens his mouth, but Jude interrupts him.

"It could be a lot more fun," Jude tells me without missing a beat, a smile spreading across his face.

I can sort of tell they're looking at each other, but I can't tear my gaze from the roguish smirk on Jude's face. It makes me burn up from head to toe. All my blood is rushing down south.

My pants were already feeling tight, after all the hot chocolate, mulled apple juice, and wine I've had to drink. But suddenly they're tight in another way completely.

I tug at my collar, unfastening the top button as I gulp.

"Truth or dare?" Jude follows up, never letting my gaze stray.

God, I want to choose dare... but I don't know if I'm brave enough.

"Truth."

Jude leans in, bracing his elbows on his knees. He gives me just the ghost of a smile, and it's so much hotter that way —so much more in control.

I already know I'm screwed.

"What's your hottest fantasy?"

Well, that's easy. I don't even have to think about the answer. But actually saying it... that's the hard part.

"I... um..." I breathe out.

All night, I've found myself so perfectly relaxed and happy around the Daddies. They tease and flirt with me constantly, but they never made me feel like I'm under a spotlight.

Now, I do. My heart is pounding against my ribcage as I stare at them like a deer in the headlights.

*What if I scare them off? What if they think it's weird?*

"Hurry up, boy," Jude tells me, rising to his feet. "Otherwise I'm gonna have to go piss."

A strangled noise escapes my throat. I stare up at him, but the power of speech is nowhere to be found.

After a few moments, the corner of Jude's lips lifts in a little smile. He leans down and presses his lips against mine, and then he heads toward the guest bathroom as I stare after him.

"Cat got your tongue?" Nye murmurs, reaching over to rest his hand on my knee. "You know we won't judge you, whatever it is." I manage the tiniest nod, and he smiles. "Good."

That's not what I'm really afraid of.

More than anything, I don't want them to be into it for all the wrong reasons. I still remember what a mindfuck it was to leave that Grindr guy's house so pleasantly satiated for the first time, yet aching with a loneliness like I'd never felt before.

If I walk out of the Behrs' front door while grappling with that same empty void in my heart…

I don't know what I'll do.

"Want to give us a hint?" Star asks. He's cross-legged on the armchair, swishing his wine glass idly as he watches me. But it's sure making a lot of noise…

No. What I hear is a trickle turning into a stream—and it's not coming from the living room.

*God help me, Jude knows exactly what he's doing.*

My gaze flickers toward the open door to the bathroom. We can't see inside from this angle, but we don't need to.

Whether I want to give them a hint or not… I just did.

"Ahhh," Nye murmurs, while Star grins at me.

I duck my head, squirming and drawing my feet up next to me. My pants are so damn tight that no position change will help me, but it's a pleasurable part of the torture in itself.

Listening to the one sound that never fails to get me hard —all the while watched by two of the Daddies—makes my brain fizz so much that I can barely form words.

I don't even know what to do now. I just want to throw myself on their mercy and beg for everything I've ever fantasized about.

"That's a good hint," Star tells me, leaning back and grinning. "But not a complete answer."

I duck my head. "It's not too weird?"

Nye chuckles. "Not even the top ten weird things we've done, collectively," he gestures between the three of them.

Relief—ironically—makes me breathe a little easier. "Really?" I murmur with a shy glance up at them.

"Really," Jude promises as he rejoins us... but isn't sitting down.

Instead, he crouches next to me, taking my empty wine glass and setting it aside. He takes both my hands and looks me in the eye, his breath warm against my cheek. "Golden," he murmurs. "Look at me."

I can't help but obey. My eyes widen as I catch his intense blue gaze, and suddenly all my squirming and embarrassment fades away into something... different.

Better.

"We want to give you everything you want," Jude says. "But there's one thing that's kept our marriage going through all these years."

"What?" I whisper.

"If any of us wants something, we have to be brave enough to ask for it." The others are watching, but I can't tear my gaze away for long enough to look at them. "It's pretty easy to read you, but none of us are psychic—except maybe Star, but that's different."

I giggle breathlessly, spellbound by every word.

"I told you before that life's like a buffet. But sometimes, you want a dish that isn't usually on the table. If you ask for it... it can get cooked up, special order. You follow me?"

I squint at him. "The metaphor's getting kind of hard to

follow." I giggle as nervous butterflies flutter around my stomach. "But… I think so."

Jude nods. "If you're going to be a good boy, you'll have to learn to ask for what you really want. Otherwise, you'll always be settling for something that isn't quite right."

Oh.

*Oh, shit. I think he might be onto something.*

I blink at Jude, my lips slowly parting. I don't even have to say it: he can tell that it home this time.

He squeezes my hands, and then he leans in to press a kiss against my lips that lingers, gathering under my skin like a steadily-building tsunami.

When he pulls away, my heart is thundering with excited anticipation.

Nye has already slid over next to me. He cups my cheek, turning my face toward him and smiling warmly before he leans in for a kiss, too. He takes his time, teasing away all my worries with playful little nips at my bottom lip until I can't help giggling.

I'm not even surprised to pull away at last and find Star already sitting on my other side, his hand tangling in the back of my hair. He holds me gently as he kisses me so deeply that my head—my whole world—starts to spin.

They're all watching me like they're waiting for an answer, and I think I know what they expect.

"I will," I whisper, looking from face to face. "I'll be a good boy. For you."

Just like that, I've earned three smiles—a smile from each Daddy. I break into a grin as Jude rises to his feet.

"Time for another bottle of wine," Jude says with a pointed look at Nye and Star. Nye ruffles my hair and Star squeezes my shoulder as they stand up, too, and head toward the kitchen.

My gaze follows them.

*Don't do it, Golden. You really shouldn't do this...*

But now that they've disappeared, I'm left all alone with my curiosity... and my need... and all my restless worry...

A minute goes by. And another.

I can't stop myself any longer. I rise to my feet and tiptoe through the living room, past the dining room, to the wine cellar and pantry. I think I can catch a fragment of their conversation through the door.

That's all I ever need: a taste.

# CHAPTER
## *Eighteen*
### JUDE

"We need to talk," I tell Nye and Star. They follow me into the pantry, and I close the door behind us. "Before this goes any further."

"Is something wrong?" Star asks.

"No. Well… yes. Not exactly."

"It's not Golden, is it?"

I sigh and shake my head. The problem isn't Golden. He's sweet. Really, *really* sweet. It's obvious how good he is for each of us, and in turn, how much we all like him.

Nye props his hands on his hips. "It's Golden."

"*No*," I snap, frowning at him.

More than anything, I want to offer him a warm respite—to trust that my weird little family is the family he's always deserved, and we can take him in from the cold.

But… I also want us to *have* him, and that scares the shit out of me.

It would mean being honest—authentic, I guess—with ourselves, with Golden, and with each other. And we've always had parts of ourselves we just couldn't bring into the relationship fully.

After more than a decade with my husbands, we all know what to expect. We're all happy enough with what we have. Introducing a boy to this delicate balance would change everything.

Yet I know for myself that some windows, once opened, can never really be closed.

"Maybe," I say at last with a sigh. "I guess I… uh… I really like him."

Star snorts. "Yeah. That checks out. Remember when we all got together? Man, you were such a dick. I haven't seen you keep your walls up like this in a long time."

I don't think about those days often, but he's probably right. I haven't been like this in a long time.

It lifts my spirits and softens my nature to have Goldie's energy around. His smile makes me want to fight back the world on his behalf when I barely even know him.

And I'm furious as hell at a world that would grind him down.

"I'm sorry," I tell them with a sigh. "But I just…" I gesture helplessly. "This shouldn't be anything new. We've been joking about this for years. *Three Daddies waiting to be old enough for their own boy.*"

Star puts his hand on my shoulder. "I was the one who said that. And it wasn't really a joke. I saw all these parts of us that we don't bring out in each other. And… well, they can't live in the dark forever."

Wait, what? I didn't even know he remembered that conversation.

"So why *now?*" I ask him, my chest tightening with worry.

I don't think he's spent the last decade unhappy… but now I'm wondering. "Why not five or ten years ago?"

Nye answers for him. "We weren't ready. I know I wasn't."

"And me," Star murmurs, and they both look at me.

I clear my throat and scuff my foot over the ground, but they aren't letting me wriggle out of this one. "Okay, fine," I sigh as each of my husbands touches one of my hands. They were right. "I've been hiding behind a… a wall."

"And this one really scares you," Nye whispers. He leans in and stretches onto tiptoe, wrapping his arms around my waist to rest his chin on my shoulder. "Tell us."

I grimace, my voice rising as I struggle to find the words. "It's just… he's younger. Obviously. He's not as experienced. He barely knows what he wants in the world. I don't even think he's had a threesome, let alone three of *us*."

Star nods and leans on the shelf next to me. "So?"

"That's fine for a plaything. It's fun for a night. But as a boy? *Our* boy? How the hell does that work?"

Both of them are silent, not saying a thing. I've never felt the need to fill the silence, but the words are spilling out of me like a dam breaking.

"We're just going to break his heart and… and toss him back out in the cold," I fling my arm out as my chest goes tight with frustration. "How can you be okay with that?"

I swear, a cool breeze sweeps through the pantry as I say those words… like a bad omen.

I keep trying to pull back—physically and emotionally—but it's too late. I've got that nagging feeling that my husbands see what I'm not saying, too. And everything that I don't see, even in myself.

Nye's chin is still planted firmly on my shoulder. "And

why do you think it's going to end that way? With us throwing him out?"

"Because..." I trail off, and my gut churns with that weird feeling of deja vu. But we've never seriously pursued a boy before.

Then my gut sinks like a stone. "Oh."

Of course it's my family.

My husbands nod. They're both smiling at me softly, sympathetically like they've been patiently waiting for me to figure it out.

I left home so long ago that I barely think about it anymore. I've poured everything into my new family—building this life with Nye and Star. Ever since we got married, I haven't had a reason to put my heart on the line. Now we do... and I never, ever want to hold us back.

I'm ready to listen to my better halves.

"So what happens now?"

Nye squeezes my hand. "Easy. We finally learn to be Daddies, just like we were always meant to be."

Yeah. That sounds right, actually.

It doesn't mean we won't make mistakes. But we can talk to each other about it—and along the way, teach Golden what real, strong love looks like.

Star jerks his thumb toward the closed door. "And we get back out there before he's old enough to need a boy of his own."

We all laugh. Star and Nye kiss while I pull a bottle of merlot out of the rack, and then they both pounce on me to take turns kissing my face until I manage to escape them and open the door.

Blanche is sitting there with an anxious look on her face, her tail thumping on the ground.

That's weird. After such a long walk, she ought to be fast asleep.

"What is it, girl?" Star asks, crouching to scratch her ears. "Oh, wait. The door's open. Did you do that?!"

Shit. I think I know what's wrong.

"Goldie? Goldie!" I call out, rushing to the front hall.

I see his coat, and his car keys… but not his boots.

Nye yanks the back door open. A gust of cold air sweeps through the room, and he shields his eyes against a flurry of snowflakes. "Guys, look!" he calls out as he crouches in the doorframe.

As I rush through the room, he turns to us. He looks so pale he might well have seen a ghost, and he's holding something up.

A pair of Christmas Bunny ears.

"Oh, fuck."

# CHAPTER

## *Nineteen*

### GOLDEN

It's my own fault.

I hunch into my sweater, bracing myself against the howling wind over the lake. But the bitter cold around me is nothing compared to the regret that numbs me to the bone.

I let my guard down. The moment I thought I could have it all, I fooled myself into believing that I can have it all without settling.

But *just right* doesn't exist.

I should have known. I *did* know, but I ignored it. I wanted to believe so badly that these Daddies could be mine.

Jude was the first one I met, and it hurts even more that it was his voice I overheard.

Just snippets, but it was enough.

*Young, inexperienced, barely knows what he wants...*

"Stupid, stupid, stupid," I grunt through chilled lips, wrapping my arms around myself as I shiver.

That wasn't the worst part, though. I'll never forget the words that followed.

*A plaything, for a night. Our boy.*

That's when I ran for home.

I only stopped for long enough to put on my boots, and right now I sure wish I'd grabbed my jacket, too. Worse still… my car is still in their driveway. I'll have to sneak back there in the early hours of the morning to pick it up.

Fuck, it's cold.

I shiver, blinking furiously. Each gust of wind drives sharp flakes straight into my eyes, and it makes it hard to see where I'm going.

Stumbling home in a blizzard, waking up alone in my plain little house on Christmas morning... *anything* beats staying at the Behr house to be used and toyed with, just for a night.

Fuck.

As frozen as I am, I can't believe the thought of being used by three Daddies is enough to automatically make my cock twitch to life. The blood stirs in my veins, shrugging off a layer of cold.

I can't let myself want this.

Why? Toys get broken. That's how Christmas morning goes. These desires are just going to get me hurt over and over.

My Christmas wish isn't for Daddies. Not anymore.

"I want to be normal," I whisper shakily. I press my numb lips together and wipe my nose, desperately trying not to cry, because I don't want the tears to freeze on my face.

Shit. It's getting dangerous out here.

I shove my hands further in my pockets and pick up the pace. I need to ignore the cold if I'm going to focus on putting one foot in front of the other. But there's nothing else on my mind besides the terrible weight crushing my heart into pieces.

I *do* want to be used.

But not like that. Not behind my back, while they say such tender things to me and act like they want to be real Daddies.

What I need is someone to see me as worthy of their claim. I want to be marked as their own, and to give them what they need in return, and to be loved so hard I can barely think straight.

In other words, everything I thought the Behrs could give me.

I can't believe I trusted them so quickly with so much of me, just because my heart told me to.

My heart is a lying liar, pants on fire.

*Or else... maybe... things aren't quite what I thought.*

But what excuse could Jude possibly have for saying—

"Shit!"

I slipped on the ice—and I'm falling.

"Ow! Fuck, that hurt!"

One hand is on the ice. I caught myself, but not in time to stop myself from making impact with the frozen surface. My wrist and knee are throbbing with pain, but the cold dulls it quickly.

Too quickly. That should definitely hurt more than it does.

I'm scared now. Really scared.

I push myself upright again, swaying against the wind as I try to shield my eyes. But however hard I squint, I can only see glimpses of light here and there through the swirling snow.

I have no idea where I am, or which way I'm going... and I'm shivering uncontrollably.

Then I hear it—a scrap of sound carried by the wind. Someone's voice. A deep voice, warm and familiar.

Help is nearby.

Another scrap of a voice, further away, and then another even closer…

It's them.

They're coming to save me.

*What if I got everything terribly, terribly wrong?*

"I'm here!" I shout out. "Over here! Help! Oh fuck—"

I slip on the ice again, and this time I don't stop the fall in time. My feet fly out from under me and I slam into the ice.

"Ow, ow, ow," I curse, and then the white blur around me gives way to a dark shape, broad shoulders.

Arms reaching down for me, scooping me effortlessly against a broad chest. Just a hint of a familiar, musky smell reaches my nose in the bitter cold, but I already know who it is.

"Daddy Jude," I whisper.

"I'm here, Goldie." With my shoulder pressed against his chest, his voice hums through me in a deep, comforting rhythm. "I've got you, boy. We've all got you." He presses his warm lips against my temple, melting away the freezing cold. "I'm so, so sorry."

But he barely needs to say a thing… the look on his face says it all. Relief, guilt, regret…

And hope.

"We're going home," Jude promises me, and I sigh and close my eyes, clutching his jacket. As I shiver against him, the world rocks and sways around me. He turns, effortlessly walking back through the storm.

Home.

I'M ALL WRAPPED UP IN A BLANKET, SETTLED ON DADDY JUDE'S lap as he sits in front of the fireplace. My other two Daddies are holding my hands, gently rubbing them between their palms.

They've stripped off my soaking wet sweater, jeans, and T-shirt. But I can't even be that horny about it, because they're talking about whether to bring me to the hospital.

As Nye raises one of my hands to inspect my chilled fingertips, I bite my lip and frown up at them all. "I-I'm fine."

Nye holds the back of my hand so tenderly against his forehead. Then, he turns my hand over and presses his lips against my palm. "Would you let us make that call, please?"

My breath catches in my throat as I meet his gaze.

I'm exhausted and freezing cold and still heartsick—the Behr Daddies could easily order me around. It means a lot that he's asking.

Despite everything, I trust them.

"Okay," I whisper, closing my eyes and nodding.

Nye squeezes my hand. "Thank you, sweetheart."

The shivers have stopped already. As I gradually warm up, I'm half-listening to them talking about how I don't have any signs of hypothermia or frostbite

"It was a close call," Jude finally murmurs. "But he'll be okay."

Star chuckles. "Doctor Blanche agrees."

She spent the first few minutes trying to slobber all over me, then making concerned whining sounds. Those have settled down too, though. When I peek through my lashes, I see her curled up on her doggy bed and ready to nap off the excitement.

"Thank God," I murmur. "Or… thank you. All of you."

They must have come straight after me to rescue me, and if they hadn't… I don't know what would have happened to me. Now that I'm back inside, I can't even see the edge of the back deck through the floor-to-ceiling windows.

"I think we all just want to know… why'd you run?" Star lets go of my hand and leans over me to kiss my forehead, then settles his weight on one hip to watch me.

My lip wobbles, and I catch my breath. I can't help looking at Jude first, and his expression creases in worry and guilt.

"Tell us. Whatever it is," he urges me.

I swallow hard. "I… um, listened in. I overheard Daddy Jude say… stuff."

"Like what?" Jude asks. He doesn't even sound a little bit mad, or defensive, or nervous. He's just watching me calmly as he cradles my head and neck in the crook of his arm. My legs are draped across his other arm, keeping me secure against his chest.

It's impossible to be nervous in the face of that overwhelming stillness and certainty. It makes me feel like I can tell him anything—even this. "That I was going to be your plaything tonight."

Jude's breath rushes out all at once. He closes his eyes and bends over, burying his face in my hair and holding me tight. "I'm so sorry," he murmurs. His thumb idly strokes the side of my neck in this tiny, affectionate gesture. "I can see what you thought. But it wasn't what I meant."

I nod, but after a few seconds, I can't figure out what he did mean. "Oh?"

Jude clears his throat and straightens up so he can look me in the eye again. "I was talking to them about how it scares me that this *isn't* just one night." For the first time, he actually looks a little bit nervous in a whole different way. Raw, perhaps. He swallows hard and looks at Nye and Star, then back at me. "Because... I'm afraid that I'll break your heart. Because I really care about you and I want to do this right."

The way he's watching me... even more than his words, it tells me that this is the truth.

"Oh," I whisper as I sigh with relief. "But... I'm still young and inexperienced. You're right. I haven't even had a threesome."

Nye runs his hand through my curls. "Getting more experience is easy," he winks.

All three of the Daddies chuckle as I blush and squirm with excitement. It's hard to stay focused on this conversation when they say things like *that*.

"But if this turns into what we all hope it does," Jude distracts me once again, "you'll always be younger than us. And that's okay."

"Not just okay. Important," Star says, while the other two nod.

"Why?"

I think I know, but I want to be sure.

Nye smiles. "Because we're all Daddies in need of a boy."

"We have been for a long time," Star says. "And somewhere along the way, we forgot that." He looks at Nye, and then Jude. It makes me smile, watching their faces soften as they look at each other. His voice is thicker as he finishes, "But we remember now. You helped us remember."

Hearing that makes me so happy I could almost cry. "Really?"

"Really," Jude whispers. "I look at you, and I see... the reason I became who I am now. So when we found you one day—today—I'll know what to do. All I have to do is trust myself."

"If you can trust yourself... then I'll trust myself, too." I smile sheepishly up at Jude, and then the others. "I shouldn't have run away. I just jumped to conclusions. I figured that maybe I was wrong about you all along. But... maybe my heart knows what it's doing, if I listen."

The three men all murmur their agreement, and Star puts his hand on my heart.

"Oh. One more thing." Jude shifts his hold on me, laying my legs down. He reaches out for something, and then I feel it on my head.

"Oh!" I reach up to confirm it's my Christmas Bunny headband. Soft, fluffy, and weird? That's definitely it. "You found it! Now, that's a miracle."

"They came off right at the back door," Nye tells me with a chuckle. "Good thing they're too big. But I have some ideas on how to resize them, if you want to."

"Really?" I gasp. "That would be amazing."

"Nothing like a Christmas morning project," Nye winks.

I blush at all the implications in his voice. The headband is already sliding to the floor just from lying here, and Nye is reaching out for it again. "Don't bother. They'll just fall off when I move around…"

"Oh? Are you planning on running away?" Jude asks me, his eyes twinkling with a self-deprecating glint.

"No," I promise, reaching up to cup his cheek in my palm.

His stubble is rough against my skin, and I love the way my fingertips rest against the side of his jaw. Even more than that, I love what it does to Jude.

He's suddenly even more focused and totally present with me, watching me like he's reading every need.

*I really hope he can.*

"Never again. I want to belong to you. All of you," I whisper, glancing between them all. "My Daddies." Then I cast him an eager glance, my cheeks flushing bright red as I squirm against the floor just a little bit.

Enough to give him a hint.

Jude smiles at me and whispers, "Our good, *good* boy."

He leans down to kiss me—tantalizingly slow, but with a heat that builds with every passing second. When he pulls away, Star is there to take over the kiss, and then Nye.

They finally give me a moment for air, chuckling as I whimper happily.

"Now, are you warm enough?" Jude murmurs.

I swallow hard as I nod. The chill in my bones—and in my heart—has thoroughly vanished. At last, I feel warm all the way through… and some parts are downright hot and hard.

Jude just raises an eyebrow.

Wait.

I've figured it out, and I can't stop my gasp.

Jude knows *exactly* what turns me on.

And he probably noticed me squirming. It's been happening more and more over the last twenty minutes. But I haven't been willing—or allowed, I think—to leave the sanctuary of my Daddies' laps.

I grin up at them all, shy and nervous and suddenly so excited I could lose my mind. "I mean… I could always be warmer." Before I can think too hard about it, I add the rest of my thought. "And… um… I've always wanted to be reminded who I belong to."

It's the boldest I've ever been, but it's like a wise Daddy once told me: if I want the special order, I have to ask for it.

Jude's eyes are sharp, intense—filled with a hunger too powerful to be contained. "Come upstairs, then," he orders.

He rises as I scramble to my feet, grabbing me by the waist. Nye and Star follow, but Jude doesn't let go. He silently steers me for every step of the way, all the way upstairs.

*I'm like the Pied Piper of Daddies.*

Instead of heading into the bedroom, Jude steers me to the en-suite bathroom before he lets go.

I only glanced at this room for a moment earlier before the bed's irresistible allure pulled me in. It's my first time really appreciating the beautiful, huge, modern room. The vanity has one long natural stone basin with two sets of matte gold taps. There's both a walk-in shower and a free-standing tub… and that sounds handy to me right now.

The heated floor is bliss on my toes as I trot to the shower. When I get to the entrance, I grin and turn around, chewing my lower lip. My nerves have come back—not because I think anything will go wrong, but because I'm so excited to finally live out my fantasies.

Nye smiles softly, reassuring me. Star is alert and attentive, his head tilted as he studies me. But Jude is the most laidback of all—and it's his calm and commanding presence that gives me strength.

He catches up to me and runs his hands gently down my sides, past my waist. He peels my underwear off—my last remaining clothing, leaving me naked and on show for all three Daddies.

Everyone can see how fucking hard I already am.

"Tell us what you want from this," Jude whispers.

"I've always wanted to be reminded who I belong to." The words almost stagger me as they leave my mouth. But there's always been something about him… I just can't help telling him the deepest truths I know.

"Show us what's ours, boy."

Holy fuck. That's the hottest thing anyone has ever said to me.

I back into the shower, my hands curling by my sides with excitement as I draw my breath and hope I get the right reaction.

"Come claim me, then."

My Daddies close in around me eagerly, all of them stripping naked.

Holy shit. I giggle as I sink to my knees on the shower floor. I sit back on my heels and lean back to show off my whole torso, resting the back of my head on the shower wall.

I feel like a precious prize they're all the happier to share.

Seeing them all naked for the first time makes this even better.

Big, broad-shouldered Jude is exactly as hairy as I

always hoped, bulging with thick muscles all over. Nye is slender, graceful, but something in the way he moves makes it clear that he's deceptively strong. And Star has the most gorgeous treasure trail, a fuzzy chest and strong thighs.

Their cocks, too… all different shapes and sizes, but all three of them are sporting a semi already.

I can't blame them. This is so hard I can't even think straight. I'm already rock-hard, my dick throbbing against my stomach.

"Look how turned on our boy is," Nye says, his voice soft with wonder, like he's excited to explore me for the first time. "And he can't stop smiling."

Oh. Oh yeah. That's why my cheeks hurt.

The Daddies crowd into the shower stall, and one by one, they take another turn kissing me.

It's torture, of the very best kind.

When I'm so desperate I can't hold out another fucking *second*, I moan and press my hands on the wall behind myself. "Now," I whimper against Jude's lips. "Please, please, *please…*"

He grins and stands up again, shoulder-to-shoulder with Nye and Star to form a semicircle.

Holy fuck.

This is already a thousand times hotter than my hottest fantasy. Because it's real, it's actually happening. They're here with me. I don't have to make up any of the details—I can see it all.

And they can see me. All of me.

I don't need to hide.

I'm so turned on and giddy with delight at being the center of all the attention, with all the thick cocks pointed toward me.

It's like waiting to be covered in their jizz... but even better.

Then it happens. I can't stop the moan of arousal when warmth streams over my body. It's like a narrow showerhead sweeping across all the spots I barely knew could be erogenous, from my nipples to my sides and hips, and—best of all —my hard dick.

Nye and Star join in. I can feel the sight burning itself into my memory forever. They're all getting hard for me, too, a silent promise of release to follow release... and all I can do is helplessly whimper and reach for myself.

"No touching," Jude orders.

I can't stop the gasp.

I didn't think I had any self-control left, but there's no doubt at all who's in charge. I can't help but obey the order. It's even hotter to be forced up against the sight of my own obedience, where I can't deny a thing.

Holy fuck.

It probably hasn't even been a minute, but it feels like an endless cumshot. It never gets any less hot—only *hotter*—as they cover my chest and stomach, sigh with relief, tip their heads back, or stroke themselves from time to time.

As their desperation eases, mine only grows.

That's the hottest part of all, knowing that they're in control of my body, my pleasure... everything. And I need to come. That's not all, either. My desperation is two-fold, too. But I need to come first, or else it's going to hurt.

But I'm not supposed to, but I *need* to...

I sag against the wall and whimper, my hands curling into tight fists as I try to resist the urge.

"Good boy," Jude murmurs. "Your best is all we can ask. It's hard. I can see that."

"We can all see that," Nye teases.

I blush furiously. It's obvious how close I am to coming hands-free.

Nye sighs and strokes himself, leaning back against the shower wall. He's finished, waiting for whatever happens next. "And we love it," Nye tells me when he sees me peeking at him. He winks. "Gold looks good on you."

"Nnngh," I moan. "It's so good. Why does it feel so hard?"

"You're giving us your pleasure, too—not just ours," Star reminds me. He squeezes his shaft, stroking out the last few droplets. "Trust your Daddies. We'll make it worth it, holding out longer."

"Okay," I whisper, peeking again. I think they're done teaching me this particular lesson, and I really hope that means I won't have to wait too much longer. "I'm sorry, Daddies. I can't help being a..." I trail off, too shy and nervous and excited.

"A greedy slut?" Jude murmurs. My eyes fly open as one last burst sprays across my chest. He strokes his cock, already hard and... intimidatingly huge. "Say it."

I giggle at the rare smile he's giving me—full of such affection that I can't even pretend to be upset.

"I'm *your* greedy slut," I whisper.

Oh, fuck, that's hot!

It takes all my self-control not to grab myself, and jerk off hard and fast. I'm quivering right on the very edge of some bliss, but my signals are so mixed-up that I can barely tell what's going to happen first.

"Show us," Star orders.

I wrap a hand around myself almost before he's done the words. "Thank you please yes thank you oh fuck—!" A few strokes, and that's enough. I'm arching, tightening, crying out… and then bliss sinks into my bones as I sink against the shower wall, covered in the evidence of my own mind-bending desire.

Maybe I'm a greedy boy, but I finally have three hungry Daddies who can indulge me. I don't have to settle for any more or less than what I want.

*Everything is just right.*

"God, you're beautiful," Jude whispers. "So… so happy."

"Mmhmm," I giggle softly. He's pulling me to my feet, turning on the shower water. He holds me from behind, like he's just waiting.

Of course he is. He knows what I need. My knees buckle with relief, and I'm finally able to let go under the watchful, kind eyes of my Daddies.

Jude wraps his hand around me, gently stroking the last few droplets out.

"Thank you," I whisper. "This was the best Christmas gift ever."

"Oh, beautiful boy," Nye chuckles, stepping up behind me so I can feel his hard-on brushing my hip. "We're just getting started."

I giggle, closing my eyes against the shower water. I feel like I'm floating away on a cloud of happiness I've only ever glimpsed.

Jude gently spreads soap all over me, and Nye's thin, strong fingers rub it into a lather. Finally, Star rinses me clean, rubbing my skin over and over until the suds finally run clean.

By the time they dry me off, all the soft touches have worked their magic, and I'm back to consciousness.

Not just that—I'm hungry again, ready for more.

I scurry to the bedroom, grinning over my shoulder. "Catch the Christmas Bunny if you can!"

I imagined my Daddies chasing me, but this is even better. They're walking slowly, yet purposefully... like they can outrun me, and they're just choosing to toy with me.

Jude corners me and pulls me into his lap on the edge of the bed, running his hands gently along every inch of my body. All three of them are studying me, memorizing everything that makes me whimper or squirm.

But it's Nye who makes me cry out. His cool, wet fingers, specifically. He chuckles, kissing my shoulder as he brushes his fingers between my thighs, around my needy little hole, and then—gently, slowly, one at a time—into me.

"Fuck," I pant, pressing my forehead into Daddy Jude's shoulders. The heat and tightness are giving way to something else... a sharp need I barely remembered, but now I can't help but focus on.

It makes my cock swell to life again.

Daddy Jude is whispering to me. "Good boy. Such a good boy. That's it. Breathe out," he orders. "Good. And in..."

I swallow hard, trembling in his lap as discomfort turns to excitement—and then ecstasy.

"Good, hm?" Star grins, sitting on the bed beside me. "You're getting hard again."

"So fucking good," I whimper. "Oh, fuck. I need... I need more."

Daddy Nye's fingers slide out of me, and just like that, Jude's tip is pressed against me.

My cheeks flush with heat. Maybe I spoke too soon. It feels like too much. I can't possibly do this. I want to—more than anything—but he's going to stuff *that* in me...?!

Jude groans, and then he pulls me toward him, and suddenly I'm yielding and giving way…

Oh, fuck. It burns and aches, stretching me past what I thought I'd ever be able to take, and he's not even all the way inside!

"Too big," I whimper. "Fuck! Fuck, I can't…"

"Shhh," Daddy Jude silences me, pressing a kiss against my lips to swallow all my words until they turn into whimpers. "That's a good boy. You can do this."

"I c—I can't—oh, fuck…!"

He slides the rest of the way inside me, and… I just lost my power of speech. I'm burning up from head to toe. I can't stop the guttural groan, even as my Daddies chuckle softly all around.

"What was that?" Daddy Jude murmurs.

"Too big!"

"Too bad." My Daddy's fingers curl around my hips, holding me so tight it feels like it'll almost bruise. And then he raises me and lowers me on his lap like I weigh nothing at all, gently pulling himself out and pushing all the way back in.

It hurts, but it's starting to hurt *really* good. My erection is trapped between our stomachs, bumping against him every time he lowers me down. And that perfect spot inside me is lighting up in a way that nothing else has ever shown me before.

God bless Daddy Jude, because however much I quiver and clench and cry out, he just keeps going at his own slow, steady pace. It's insanely hot, being used like a fucktoy while he kisses me and tells me what a good boy I'm being, and how proud and happy he is…

When he finally loses control, he slams himself into me so

deep that all the nerves in my body sing at once. He's claiming me from the inside out, leaving me dripping wet as he grunts and holds me down on his cock until the last possible moment.

Fuck. He's pulling me off his lap.

I'm so turned on it hurts, and I feel so empty inside now… but I know that won't be a problem for long.

It's Daddy Nye's turn now.

I gasp and press my face into the bed as he straddles me and slips inside. He's nowhere near as big as Jude, meaning I'm no longer clawing at the border between pain and pleasure.

The relief of catching my breath is subsiding, though. I moan with frustration, spreading my legs and pushing back into Nye. "I—I need more."

"I'm too small, huh?" Nye murmurs with such deceptively sweet sympathy.

I pause, my breath catching with excitement. Something in his voice is… almost delighted, like he's just waiting to share a secret with me.

"Don't worry, sweet boy. I waited 'til after Jude so I can do… *this.*"

He yanks me back to the edge of the bed until my feet are on the floor, and grabs the curls at the back of my head.

"Oh my—*oh!*" I cry out as he drives into me again. "Oh, oh, ahhh, nngh!" He's going hard and fast. It's been seconds, and I'm not only turned on again… I'm soaring right past the peak, into a whole new plane of arousal.

My thighs are trembling, but he's got me so firmly pinned against the bed that I can barely move. The duvet isn't enough friction for my hard cock, but I can't even hope to reach myself—and my hands are on his wrists as he yanks me back by my hair.

It feels so fucking *good*.

My hoarse, throaty moans are picking up to a fever pitch. I don't know if I can come hands-free, but I think I'm going to find out soon. Nye is covering my shoulders in sweet little kisses, but he never stops mercilessly using me.

I'd like to say I've learned my lesson, but I want him to teach me this lesson *many* more times.

"Daddy!" I cry out as his pace finally breaks its rhythm. "Fuck…! Yes please, fuck, keep going, it's so good…!"

Nye groans, grabbing my shoulders with both hands as he finishes deep inside me. I love the thought that he's adding his load to Jude's, but I know they won't let me rest until all three of them have shared me.

"Holy fuck. Golden," Nye pants as his hips shudder a few final times. "You're—you're a *very* good boy."

I can't help a happy little giggle, mixed with a whimper—because I'm clinging to the edge of another orgasm, and my whole world might fall apart if I don't have another cock inside me pronto.

My knees give way and I slide a little down, but Star grabs me and hoists me up. Not just onto the bed, but all the way into his arms, face-to-face.

I wrap my arms and legs around him, burying my face in his shoulder at the now-familiar heat of being stretched open by a new cock.

"Ohhh," I groan as he sinks all the way into me. His cock is just the right length to hit the spot inside me perfectly with every thrust, and I already know I'm not going to last long.

My fingers and toes curl as I whimper, trying to move with him and push myself down onto his cock in this perfect rhythm. Thrust after thrust sends me closer to the edge. I don't know how long I've been slamming deeper onto his cock, because time itself doesn't matter anymore.

All that matters is *us*. Me and my Daddies.

"I knew the moment I saw you," Star whispers, "I knew you'd be our perfect boy."

Every taut muscle in my body clenches just a little bit more… and then all the pent-up energy in both of our bodies releases all at once.

Blackness. Bliss, more complete and all-consuming than I've ever known. Warm hands. A hot shower, and more soap all over me, a gentle washcloth, a soft bath towel.

Kisses on my forehead, cheeks, shoulders.

"Fuck," I breathe out, blinking sleepily. We're all in bed together, curled up in a giant pile. I'm lying with my head in Jude's lap. Nye is holding me from behind, and my face and curled-up hands are tucked against Star's chest.

"That was a good fuck?" Star whispers, stroking my hair.

"The best fuck I've ever dreamed of," I mumble, and my Daddies chuckle. "I'm so happy. It feels *so* good."

"Good," Jude tells me softly, his fingertips playing with my curls. "Because you deserve everything you've ever dreamed of."

I smile, and something's coming back to me. But this tiny shred of reality doesn't disturb the perfect little bubble I'm floating in.

"I applied for the interior design program… to become a Christmas decorator."

Jude catches his breath. "You did?"

"Yeah," I whisper, glancing at Nye and Star. "It's the only thing I've ever wanted to do. But it's time to believe in myself a little more, and… to stop assuming I can't, before I even try."

They all smile at me.

"Find your special order," Jude murmurs.

I giggle. "Speaking of special orders… do I get a reward?" I squirm against them all, well aware that Nye's cock is tucked between my thighs, and Star's is resting against mine, and Jude's—well, that's right in front of my eyes.

"You will," Jude growls, playfully ruffling my curls. "Unlimited sausage for good boys."

Star cups my cheek as he smiles at the three of us. "But, even more than that… the same promise we made each other when we first got together. All the love you could ever want."

*Love?* I quiver silently, staring at them all. *Is that—should I —what do I—oh my god.*

"We're not going to rush into saying it," Nye says. Even I can hear him scolding Star right now, and I join in their laughter.

Star boops my nose and then rolls his eyes at Nye. "Yes, Daddy." When we're done laughing, though, he's still gazing at me with these eyes that are all soft and full of wonder. "But… when you know, you know. And we've been waiting a lifetime."

I blush, shyly biting my lip. "I've never been in love before. And I'm just getting to know you. But… I think I'm falling for all of you."

It makes me catch my breath to say it aloud, because it feels so true—and so new. My smile must be glowing like a Christmas tree.

"But," I add hastily, "I won't rush into saying anything either. In fact," I add, raising my chin and clicking my tongue, "I plan to make you all work for it. So there."

They all chuckle softly.

"That's our good boy," Jude murmurs. "We have nothing but time."

I peek through my lashes again in time to see the Daddies exchanging a look. And this time, I feel like I *might* just know what this one says…

Star smiles, catching my gaze as he speaks for them all.

"Our perfect golden boy."

"Is that all the presents?"

After the past year, I'm fully aware of what a compromising position I'm in. On all fours, my head fully under the Christmas tree... I'm practically begging for a Daddy to come along and take advantage of the situation.

"Yeah, it is," I say, answering my own question.

But Jude just wraps his arm around my waist and hauls me out out of there, and up onto the sofa.

Good thing Nye fixed my Christmas Bunny ears last year. They stay firmly in place despite all the manhandling—which is good, because I've had a lot of it this year.

"Oh, no, it isn't," Jude corrects me. "There's one more."

I laugh and wriggle against him as he pulls me right up into his lap on the sofa. "If you say so, Daddy. You're always right."

Not only have I gotten into the interior design program of my dreams, but I've accumulated quite a social media following already. I've been invited to collab with several big brands in the last few months alone, and I'm scheduled to have lunch with my first magazine editor in the New Year.

It's been six months since I moved into the Behr house—right after Ellie finally found the right person to keep up with her, and they bought out the coffee shop together.

And in that time, I gotta say, I've been delighted to get used to this. Even when I'm studying on the sofa, there's often a Daddy around who knows exactly what I need—and is prepared to interrupt me to deliver it.

"So, where is it?" I ask Jude, looking around for presents.

Blanche whines and paws at my knee. I almost get up to let her outside… and then I look a little closer.

There's something tied to her collar. A tiny, gift-wrapped box, in fact.

My lips part as I look around at my Daddies. "Is that…?"

"I think it says *To Goldie, from your Santas,*" Jude pretends to read it out loud.

"I think it was *supposed* to say that, but *someone* forgot to pick up the gift tags," Nye murmurs, and I snicker. "Honestly, I don't know why I bothered wrapping it. It's not like you haven't seen it."

My lips part, and I furrow my brows. I know about the rings Nye gave the other Daddies last Christmas. They got them resized months ago, and they've been wearing them ever since.

So what's this?

I have to dodge a lot of Blanche slobber, but I finally manage to get the box from her collar.

"Here you go," Star laughs and tosses Blanche her Christmas gift—a huge bone. "That should distract her for at least three minutes."

I hastily tear the paper off the little jewelry box, and I even manage to open it despite my trembling hands.

There are three rings, and they look just like the Daddies' rings: gold, silver, and rose gold.

"You… bought more?"

"These are the originals," Nye tells me quietly. "Before we got them resized, I measured your finger while you were asleep."

I manage a little giggle. "In my sleep? Weird."

"Not at all weird. Not like breaking into someone's house —" Jude starts. He just laughs against my mouth when I kiss him to shut him up.

"And it just so happens that there *is* one person they fit."

A chill runs down my spine. "No way."

Jude smiles and takes the box from me, plucking the gold ring out of it. He hands the box to Nye, then takes me by the hand. "Golden—our beautiful golden boy. Thank you for having faith in me—and giving me my faith back, when I thought it was long gone. Thank you for teaching me who I am, and reminding me what I'm supposed to be. It would be the greatest honor of my life—for the second time over—" he smiles at the Daddies, "if you'd be ours. Forever."

"Oh, my god," I murmur through the tears. "Yes. Fuck. Of course."

He slides the gold ring on my finger, and then it's Nye's turn.

"Oh, Golden," he whispers, kissing my forehead and taking my hand. "I've loved getting to know you from the inside out." The other men laugh, and he smacks them both, making me giggle. "Hey. I'm trying to be serious, for a change. Right. Where was I?"

"Inside me," I giggle.

Nye bursts out laughing. "Yes. And also… oh, fuck it," he tosses his head back dramatically. "I give up. Golden, you've stolen the piece of my heart I never knew I was saving for you. Please—be ours."

I'm a little more ready this time, but not by much. "*Fuck yes.*" I dab my cheeks as much as I can with one hand as he slides the silver ring on.

Finally, it's Star who takes my hand with a quiet smile. "Golden. I barely had to say two words before I knew the universe had delivered everything we've ever needed. I've been waiting a long time for you, and… let me say, you've blown away every expectation I ever had. Will you be ours?"

"*Yes,*" I whisper, my voice cracking as he slides the third, and final, ring onto my finger.

I don't know how to find the words to tell them everything… but all I have to do is tearily blink at them, and I think they know.

"Thank you, Santa. And all Santas," I giggle. "You really did bring me my Christmas miracle."

# About the Author

E. Davies writes feel-good, low-angst romance that never fades to black when the going gets good! Born in Canada, after 16 moves and counting, Ed has finally put down roots in north London.

He emerges from his writing nest to coo over fuzzy animals, flee from cute guys, dance through the streets with his chosen family, put together fierce looks, and—most of all—befriend local flowers.

### FOLLOW E. DAVIES ONLINE:

amazon.com/author/edavies
bookbub.com/authors/e-davies
facebook.com/edaviesauthor
goodreads.com/edavies
instagram.com/edaviesauthor

*Also by E. Davies*

## SUNRISE ISLAND BROTHERS

Collide, Stranded, Adrift, Unmoored

## TWISTED

Golden Boy, Beauty Sleep

## HART'S BAY

Hard Hart, Changed Hart, Wild Hart, Stolen Hart

## SIGNIFICANT BROTHERS

Splinter, Grasp, Slick, Trace, Clutch, Tremble

## RILEY BROTHERS

Buzz, Clang, Swish, Crunch, Slam, Grind

## BROOKLYN BOYS

Electric Sunshine, Live Wire, Boiling Point

## F-WORD

Flaunt, Freak, Faux, Forever, Freedom

## AFTER

Afterburn, Afterglow, Aftermath

## SHARED UNIVERSES

**Rosavia Royals:** Barely Regal

**Men of Hidden Creek:** Shelter, Adore, Miracle, Redemption

**Vino & Veritas:** Limelight

## AND MORE...

For a complete list of available titles by E. Davies:

edaviesbooks.com/books